Mrs. Mackenzie Daniel

Reaping the Whirlwind

Vol. III

Mrs. Mackenzie Daniel

Reaping the Whirlwind
Vol. III

ISBN/EAN: 9783337249991

Printed in Europe, USA, Canada, Australia, Japan

Cover: Foto ©Andreas Hilbeck / pixelio.de

More available books at **www.hansebooks.com**

REAPING THE WHIRLWIND.

A NOVEL.

IN THREE VOLUMES.

BY

MRS. MACKENZIE DANIEL,

Author of "After Long Years," "Miriam's Sorrow," "My Sister
Minnie," "Our Guardian," &c.

VOL. III.

London:

T. CAUTLEY NEWBY, PUBLISHER,
30, WELBECK STREET, CAVENDISH SQUARE.
1864.

REAPING THE WHIRLWIND.

CHAPTER I.

META'S ANTECEDENTS.

My mother came out of the breakfast-room into the hall as we entered the house—came to meet us and stop us from going on to where Meta had taken refuge, and had made mamma hastily promise she should be left in peace.

"She is tired and unwell, poor child! and shrinks from seeing a stranger at present. Mr.

Wyke will understand this, Ethel, and excuse me for a minute or two while I get Meta some refreshment. Go to the drawing-room, my love, and presently I will join you there."

"The wisdom of the serpent!" I said, as we went the way we were bidden without so much as a murmur; "she will manage to twine herself round mamma again, and induce her to believe that black is whiter than snow. When will you tell me all you know about this strange relative of ours, Mr. Wyke?"

"Now, if you please," he said, first finding me an easy chair, and assuring himself that my paleness was only the result of the morning's agitation. "I detest secrets very cordially, and shall be glad to have a sharer in the one of which four years ago I was made the sole depositor. Now and always, my darling Ethel shall know whatever I know, and help my judgment in any difficult matter with her own."

I need not repeat what I said in answer to this. Perhaps the reader is already somewhat tired of me and my courtship, and will be glad to have for a change Mr. Wyke's narrative of his acquaintance with my cousin, and with those facts in her early history which she had hitherto succeeded so well in concealing from us.

I will give the story in the vicar's own words, as they were both brief and to the point. Here it is:

"Four years ago I was staying at Heidelberg for my health. I had taken up my quarters at the least fashionable hotel I could hear of, and without knowing that any of my countrypeople were located there before me. As a rule, I prefer not meeting and becoming familiar with English people when I am abroad. The second day, however, of my residence in the house, as I sat one morning at breakfast, there came a gentle and rather timid knock at my door, followed, as soon as

I had said 'Come in,' by the entrance of a young girl looking excessively pale and frightened. I just saw this, and also that my visitor was unquestionably a lady, when, in a quick, agitated voice, and speaking in tolerable English, she made known the object of her visit. 'You are a clergyman,' she said —'the master of the hotel has told me so. My husband is dying upstairs—he also is English; will you come to him?' I asked no questions, gathering from the girl's manner that the case was urgent, but followed her at once to her husband's presence. A doctor had just left him, they told me, and exhausted by the effort of answering questions, the poor young man was lying back almost senseless, on his pillows, and seeming, as far as I could judge, very near death indeed. The wife approached the bed, and in a low voice offered him some medicine. He opened his eyes, saw me behind her, and instantly swallowed the draught. 'Now leave us for half an hour,' he said, addressing the pale girl bending over him, 'I must talk to this countryman of mine alone.' The wife obeyed in perfect silence, and I turned from closing the door upon her, to find myself face to face with the dying man. After a few general expressions of sympathy with his evident sufferings, I asked my young countryman if I should pray with him, or if he desired first to say anything to me in reference to his last wishes. 'My time is short,' he replied, in a labouring voice, 'and I have much to say that, if left unsaid, would haunt me, even in the grave. God knows I have urgent need of a good man's prayers, but I must speak first, and then you shall do what you will. See that the door is closed tight. Some ears can hear even through stone walls.'

" It was a long and very mournful story that he then told me. I will shorten it to you, Ethel, as much as I can, lest we should be interrupted before I arrive at the close. His name was

Alan Beresford, and he had been living abroad for several years. No very near connections remained to him—two maiden aunts were the only ones he knew of except the Earl of Clinton, to whose title and estate he was the heir. Rather more than two years prior to the time of our meeting, he had become acquainted with a very fascinating German girl, who was employed as daily governess in a family where he visited. The admiration she inspired soon ripened into a profound attachment which the young lady appeared to share. After awhile he proposed marriage to her, without, however, giving her a hint as to the earldom in prospective. He was evidently of a very ardent, romantic nature, which made him desire earnestly to be loved for himself alone. The young lady consented to become his wife on the condition of their marriage being kept secret for a time. Her German friends, she said, would not approve of her uniting herself to so young a man (I forgot to mention that Mr. Beresford was a year younger than his wife), and who as yet had no definite position in the world. This arrangement was quite as agreeable to the gentleman as to the lady. He knew that his friends would severely censure an alliance between the future Earl of Clinton and a poor German governess, however beautiful and attractive she might be. So he took her to England, and married her in an obscure country village, with no witnesses except the clerk and the old woman who swept out the church and opened the pews. After this they returned to Germany, his income being insufficient to provide a home for them in England; and here they had remained, though not always in the same place, ever since. 'I am now dying,' he continued, having, in a rapid, excited manner, given me this brief sketch; 'and looking upon you as the Catholics look upon their confessors, I tell you that the woman I married, and whom you have just now seen, has been my death. Not by poison ' (for I suppose I had started as he said this), 'not by any means that could bring trouble upon herself, but by a coldness that has frozen my very heart, by a lightness that has outraged every feeling of propriety in which, as an Englishman, I was educated; by a vanity so extraordinary and insatiable that, had it been any other than my own wife who displayed it before me, I should have studied it as the greatest curiosity in the shape of a human weakness ever brought under my notice. I believe that my wife is what the world calls pure. I am making no accusation against her that would injure her character in the eyes of society— but for myself I have lost all faith, all confidence, all hope in the woman I have so passionately loved.   With a vanity like hers that will be fed, no matter how coarse the food within its reach, I would never answer for her future destiny ; and now for the reason of my troubling you, a stranger, with this sad and dreary lament of a lost and wasted life. We have a child, a little boy, who, on my death, will become the Earl of Clinton's heir. His mother never cared for him as I did. Her affection seemed to come by fits and starts—she would neglect him at any time for a party of pleasure, where she expected to gain the admiration for which she daily sells her soul. I could not bear this, even while I was 'vely well and strong myself. ' child, only less madly th᷍ ᷍᷍᷍er, but I took him away ᷍r old, and committed him to tᴅ. maiden aunts I told you of. They are pious, charitable creat ᷍es, and they believe, as I made them do, that they are fostering a child of shame, for whi᷍᷍ ᷍ood deed they will receive their reward in ano᷍ ᷍r worl᷍᷍᷍ ᷍ ᷍ my return, when Meta passionately ᷍ ᷍rily reproached me for robbi᷍ what sh᷍ called then her only comfort, I told her that she was not my lawful wife. You, as a clergyman, may condemn me for this lie, but you cannot enter into the bitter, bitter, heartbreaking emotions which suggested it. I knew by that time, or suspected, that I had not long to live, and I dared not—do you understand me?—I dared not leave my name and honour to the mercy of a woman who would pass by the open gates of paradise—knowing that they would never open for her again—if a worshipper of her beauty stood beyond. I cannot linger on the time that followed this; suffice it that, in her total ignorance of English laws and customs, she believed me; and dating from that day our life together has been more wretched than words can tell. She would have left me but that I assured her I was doomed to death, and reminded her that but for her I might have lived a long and happy life. I think, now that it has come to the last, she is frightened, and a little softened towards

me ; but my resolution is unshaken. At my
death she will have all I can leave her, which
is little enough, as I have had the misfortune
to belong to the very poorest branch of the
family, which boasts an earl for its head. She
will resume her maiden name, and, without
the incumbrance of the child I have taken from
her, will no doubt do very well for herself.
And now for my last solemn request and
charge to you, who have surely been sent
as a special mercy to me in my dying hour.
I shall give you the name and address of those
relatives of mine who have my little boy in
their keeping. Should he be alive at the time
of the present Earl of Clinton's decease, you
will seek him out, and, making all this statement public, claim for him his title and estates.
In an event like this, where the child's future
is involved, I must set aside the chances of
his mother having acted foolishly, in the
meanwhile—but he is a very delicate boy, and
I think there is a greater likelihood of his

dying in infancy, than living to succeed the present earl. You will put yourself in correspondence with his guardians, and thus learn how matters turn out. Should he die while the earl yet lives, your trouble and responsibility will at once be at an end. In the other case, you understand now my wish, and, as it is the last and most solemn wish of a dying man, you will not fail to perform it. A copy of our marriage certificate, with the address I have spoken of, shall be ready for you by this evening, when I beg you will come in and see me again. Now I am very faint and exhausted, and must be left for a while alone.'

" ' One question only,' I said, as he ceased speaking, and as something in his face assured me that there would be little more time given him on earth—' do you feel, on the brink of eternity, that you are justified in leaving your lawful wife under the impression that she has been your mistress, living with you in sin, at any rate since you told her the marriage was not legal, and forfeiting all claim to the respect and consideration of those around her? Do you think that she is less likely to realize your fears about her conduct, by believing herself already lost, than if she knew she had a right to the sacred names of wife and widow?'

"'She is less likely to dishonour my name,' he said excitedly, 'and every man, living or dying, has a right to protect that.'

"'But not to sacrifice truth and justice for it,' I added firmly. 'Pray think this matter over calmly and dispassionately when I leave you. We will talk of it again to-night.'

"'Do you refuse, then, to serve me in the way I have pointed out?' he cried, raising himself in his bed, weak as he was, and trembling with an angry emotion that I feared would destroy him. 'Speak—speak at once! Your hesitation will kill me.'

"I said, after a minute's reflection, 'I will

do all you require of me, except assist in deceiving your wife—that I cannot do. Tell her the truth, and exact, if it must be so, a promise that she will not claim her name until the Earl of Clinton dies and it becomes necessary to establish the rights of your child. Tell her to shape her conduct as becomes the mother of a future earl, and—'

"I could not conclude my sentence, for, looking up as I heard a smothered groan, I saw that the poor young man had fallen back on his pillows in a fainting fit.

"The wife came in immediately upon my ringing the bell, and, as far as I could judge, devoted herself both zealously and kindly to her dying husband. As he opened his eyes, after an interval of some minutes, she bent over him and whispered, ' Poor, poor Alan !' Then I left them together, and heard nothing more of them till, rather late that night, I was summoned by the landlord hastily to their room.

"Mr. Beresford was almost at his last when I stood once more beside his bed, but he had strength the instant he saw me to draw a triply-sealed envelope from beneath his pillow, and to put it in my hands. 'Unchanged, unchanged,' was all he could gasp out, and then the wife, whose face was ashey pale now, asked me if I would pray, as she thought it might comfort him. So I knelt by the unhappy sufferer—she kneeling on the other side of me—and prayed that his departing soul might even at this eleventh hour find light and peace. God only knows how it really was with him, for he died and made no sign ; and then I rose and carried the wife, hysterical and fainting, into another room, and called the landlady to remain with her. Ethel, I had firmly resolved to see her the next day and tell her the whole truth. I did not think she quite deserved her husband's harsh judgment, and even had she done so I could not have deceived her. But it was not to be. The next morning, when I sent to inquire how she had passed the night, the answer was brought me that Mrs. Beresford had left the hotel by daybreak, and that nobody had the least notion whither she had gone. For a whole month I caused the most diligent inquiries to be made, and I advertised in half the German papers, without success. She had left sufficient money with the landlady (who I sometimes fancied was in her confidence), to provide a decent funeral for her husband, but she had been content that strangers should lay him in his lonely grave. This, I must confess, gave me a worse opinion of her than anything that poor young man had told me, and by degrees I ceased to think anxiously of her at all. On returning to England I ascertained that her child was alive, and still safe in the care of his elderly relatives in Devonshire. From time to time they write to me (as a supposed friend of both his parents) to assure me of his health and safety, but until yesterday, when you enlightened me as to the connection between the Hallams and the Earl of Clinton, my interest in the whole affair had been slumbering for a considerable period. That my Meta and your Meta should be the same individual, appears too strange to be true, and yet I never, never could be mistaken in that peculiar face, little as I saw of it ; and now I remember having once been startled by your cousin's voice, and telling you that it brought to my mind a voice I had heard under painful circumstances in Germany, some years before. Ethel, she must not escape me again. You think she will remain here for the present ?"

" I think she came with that intention, certainly," I replied, my brain still dizzy with the effort I had made to follow the vicar in his rapid narrative, " but that she is most anxious to shun you, I have learnt before today, and there is no knowing what she may do if she believes you have discovered her. Hitherto she has trusted to your habit of never looking into a woman's face—you know this was your habit when you first came to Graybourne—but under the improved state of things which exists at present, Meta will probably consider flight her only remedy. We must be prompt in whatever is to be done, for I have every reason to believe an engagement of some kind has been contracted between herself and Edmund Hallam."

" Monstrous! cruel!" exclaimed the good vicar, indignantly; " she deserves whatever that ill-fated husband of hers condemned her to suffer, but Alicia must not be a victim; this unhallowed engagement which you suppose has been entered into, must be dissolved at once. Your mother is long in coming, Ethel.   Shall we wait, or will you go and ask your cousin to grant me an interview as soon as she is rested?"

I was on the point of saying that I doubted

the utility of making such a request without letting her first understand what it was that Mr. Wyke had to say to her, when mamma, looking very pale and agitated, suddenly entered the room.

" I could not come sooner," she said, hurriedly, " and now I must send Ethel to her cousin, while I remain here for a few minutes. Meta is very ill ; she has undergone great excitement lately. I have not a word to urge in justification of her conduct, my love" (this was to me), " but while her bodily health demands our care, it would be useless, as well as cruel, to reproach her. I left her nearly fainting on my bed; will you go to her ?"

" And in the meanwhile, dear," said Mr. Wyke, as he opened the door for me, and clasped my hand for a moment, " I had better give your mother an outline of the strange story I have been telling you. It may in some degree modify the compassion she appears disposed to lavish upon this dangerous young woman. You will come back to me presently ?"

" As soon as I can. If I find Meta capable of listening, shall I prepare her for what you have to communicate ?"

" Tell her the whole if you can, and thus spare her the pain of seeing me at all. I leave everything to you, dearest; only be quick, as I shall want you to have a little walk with me before I return home."

So I left him with my mother, and hastened to the room where Meta was taking rest—too really exhausted at present in mind as well as body to care greatly who it was that ministered to her.

CHAPTER II.

WIFE AND MOTHER.

THERE was nothing to be done in the way of questions or communications as regarded Meta at present. Her bodily illness was a thing neither to be disputed nor neglected, and so until mamma returned to the room (she was not long absent), I contented myself with chafing my cousin's icy fingers, and bathing her temples with lavender water. Once, when she had revived a little under this treatment, she held my hand fast, and drew me down till my face was close to her own.

"Ethel, is it true that you are going to marry Mr. Wyke?" she asked, with eager excitement in her voice.

"Yes," I said; "quite true; we should have written to tell you of it, if you had not so unexpectedly arrived. I only knew it myself two days ago."

"Did he recognise me just now?"

This was in a lower and fainter tone, for her strength was fast going again. I did not want to increase her agitation, so I replied, evasively—

"Meta, you have nothing to fear from Mr. Wyke. Oh, you cannot imagine how good he is."

"It is precisely his goodness that I do fear," she said, with as much energy as her weakness would permit, "do tell me the truth, at once, Ethel."

Fortunately for both of us, mamma opened

the door at that instant, and coming up to the
bed with a basin of some light soup in her
hand, told me she would take my place, as
the vicar was waiting for me.

"I must see you by and bye, Ethel, when
I am a little better," Meta called out as I
was turning away, without speaking to her.
"Promise me to come back, and do what I
have asked you."

" Yes, yes, I promise," was my hasty reply;
for, in the state she had worked herself into,
I was afraid to utter a word that might increase the excitement of her mind, and I
knew mamma would get her to sleep if possible before I should see her again. "I shall
be home in an hour's time, Meta."

" And in the meanwhile," my mother said,
speaking as kindly and tenderly as ever,
" this poor child must have all the rest she
can get. I will look after her."

I wondered, as I went gladly back to the
drawing-room, that mamma's great love for

Guy, and fears as to how Meta's conduct would affect him, did not wring out of her heart every drop of pity for the girl who had so recklessly trifled with his happiness, as well as with the happiness of everybody who came between her and her selfish projects. It was not till some time after that I learnt to understand the secret of this devoted mother's forbearance and magnanimity.

I had a delightful walk with Mr. Wyke in the same fields to which he had taken me two evenings before, but which would never again, I thought, look quite as they had looked that night with the golden sunlight casting such a glory over them and the tall elms flinging down their cool shadows on the waving grass. We spoke much of my cousin and her past life; a little of Maggie and the wonders that sea air with my love and my nursing were to do for her. Somewhat of our own future, which, in as far as our mutual affection was concerned, was to be apart and distinct from everything else, and be independent of all the accidents and changes of this changing world, so long as a gracious God should spare us each to the other.

And finally we spoke of Gertrude.

"I think," Mr. Wyke said—"that Walter has more than a passing admiration for your sister, and every day I am more and more disposed to believe him what he professes to be. If you have any idea, Ethel, that Gertrude is otherwise than momentarily interested in this friend of mine, I can see no reason for her shunning him as you say she appears resolved on doing."

"My own impression is," I told him, "that she despises herself for giving Mr. Kenyon a second thought; that even were she sure he cared for her seriously (which she is not), she would still struggle desperately against the promptings of her heart in the matter. It seems to her that love and earnest work are quite incompatible, and having in the beginning so emphatically declared her choice of the last, and her contempt for the first, she would almost rather die than confess she had failed, and failed so early, in her steadfast purpose. Something too she knows, or guesses, in which Lizzie Vivian is concerned, and I am sure her belief is that if she withdraws altogether from Mr. Kenyon's society he will eventually console himself and make Lizzie happy by marrying her. Anyhow, it is certain that Gertie will please herself, and her pleasure just now is to drive sentiment and Walter Kenyon out of her head by hard work—to try at least to do it. Time will show how far the experiment will succeed."

"You at least are not sanguine as to the result;" said Mr. Wyke with a smile—"hard work would not be your method of curing yourself of a weakness you were ashamed of ?"

"Yes, it would," I replied gravely. "If you had married Miss Dora, I should very soon have hired myself out as a washerwoman, and rubbed all the skin off my fingers, as a homœopathic method of curing my heart-ache."

I did not intend to give him an excuse for caressing and pitying the fingers alluded to, but as I had paid him so high a compliment, I suppose he felt himself bound to acknowledge it in some way. After this, he agreed with me that it would be best to allow my sister to go on in her own course for as long as she felt that course to be the right one, and not to seek, either directly or indirectly, to bring her and Mr. Kenyon together.

" And yet," the vicar acknowledged, as we walked slowly homewards, " if this young man is what I now judge him to be, I should like extremely to see him your sister's husband. I should like it for her sake—believing as I do that woman's most natural and most successful work is ever performed in a home of her own, on behalf of her husband and children—and for his sake, because, with all his so-called friends, he appears to me really friendless—and because I think I detect in his character a want of strength and firmness, which a wife like Gertrude would supply. I am greatly interested in Walter still, you see, Ethel, and cannot bear the idea of his being cast out again on a world so full of temptations to all evil."

"The virtue," I said somewhat arrogantly—" that will not stand temptation, can be worth very little. My Gertie, at any rate, is much too good for a man who only walks in a straight path as long as there is a hedge on either side of him to prevent him from getting into a crooked one."

" Child, child!" exclaimed Mr. Wyke, laying his hand in very tender rebuke on mine—" don't you know that we should all run into crooked paths, every day and every hour of our lives, if a hedge that we cannot break through, because it is planted by omnipotence, did not keep us walking in the narrow way ?

Temptations are not so easily resisted that we should judge harshly those who yield to them, or spare any pains to help our fellow men from becoming the victims of their natural weaknesses."

I only pressed the kind hand of the friend I was ever learning increasingly to honour, in token that I accepted the reproof, but inwardly I determined to remember and, if possible, act upon it, when I came to discuss the past and the future, face to face, with my cousin Meta.

Gertrude received the news of our cousin's arrival and illness very coldly, and expressed no desire whatever to see her. We communicated to her what we had heard from Mr. Wyke on the subject of Meta's past history, and while she agreed with us that it was a tale both strange and sad, she did not seem interested in discussing it, nor at all curious as to any of its details.

" If you can manage to save Alicia," she remarked, " from a participation in the miseries this girl appears destined to create around her, you will have done a good work. For Meta herself, I have no pity, and little hope, and the sooner we get rid of her altogether, the better it will be for us. I suppose when she knows she is the mother of a future earl, she will not care for the countenance or protection of her insignificant relations at Lindenhurst."

It always appeared to me that in proportion as my sister grew hard and unsympathising towards anyone who had displeased her, my heart softened to the unhappy individual, no matter how grave the offence committed might have been. There was something in Gertrude's hardness and coldness, when she *was* cold and hard, that struck me as peculiarly calculated to terrify and depress the object of her anger, and hence it was, I suppose, that any indignation of my own, against the sin of the offender, dwindled into compassion for the result which the offence had entailed.

Meta slept during all the time we were at dinner, and for nearly two hours after. Then, awaking refreshed, with strengthened nerves, she rang her bell, and entreated that I would go to her.

" You will be very cautious and very gentle, my dear, I know," said mamma, as I rose to obey the summons; " remember what a bitter trial this unfortunate girl has had to pass through since the day her husband told her that falsehood. A proud woman, who believes she has been betrayed and deceived, must be judged leniently for almost any amount of recklessness."

" I will not forget," I replied, while some other words recently listened to, mingled with what mamma had said, and inclined me to feel very tenderly and very charitably towards this poor, erring Meta.

She was sitting up by an open window when I went in, and looking, except for one burning spot on her pale cheeks, much as usual. I took a chair beside her, asked her a few general questions about her health just to show her that I had the same cousinly interest in her as ever; and then, before she had time to repeat the inquiry she had made in the morning about Mr. Wyke's recognition of her, told her the whole story I had heard from him, with the addition of his earnest wish that I should make her real position known to her.

Meta listened to all the beginning of this too familiar narrative with scarcely any external signs of emotion. Her lips might have become a little more compressed, and the red on her cheeks a shade or two brighter, but there were no exclamations, no comments, no attempts to interrupt me—until I arrived at her husband's confession of the fraud he had practised on her, with his alleged motives for inflicting on his lawful wife such manifestly cruel pain.

At this point her interest and excitement became quite beyond her power to conceal, though I am sure it was wormwood to that proud spirit to be obliged to betray to me the inward workings of her bruised heart on the subject of those wrongs she had hitherto had strength and courage to bear alone.

Quite apart from my resolution to be tender and indulgent towards this really unhappy girl, I could not but sympathise heart and soul with the almost overpowering agitation excited by what I was telling her. Vain, weak, frivolous—even heartless, to some extent, she might be—but she was not impure, and for more than four weary years she had believed herself a mother and not a wife, an l so believing had resolutely trampled down every sweet and holy feeling of motherhood, ignoring the very existence of her child, because the alternative would have entailed the exposure of her shame, and she felt she should have grown to hate the innocent evidence of it.

Something of this she expressed to me, in

a half wild, passionate manner, then, adding a storm of bitter words—truths they might have been, but if so they were hard truths to be spoken by the living of the dead—concerning the husband who, even in their last solemn parting scene, had not relented towards her.   But though I was really curious to hear Meta's own version of the sad story of her married life, I dared not allow her to enter upon any lengthy explanation yet.   A very little more excitement would, I knew, suffice to bring on an attack even worse than that of the morning; and there were deeper interests attached to the future, and which claimed more immediate attention, than any belonging solely to the past.

First of all, I must discover the real nature of that suspected engagement between my cousin and Edmund Hallam which was threatening (if it had not already accomplished), the overthrow of poor Alicia

Clarkson's happiness, and doubtless entailing upon the infatuated young man a hopeless estrangement from his family.

I asked Meta the question point blank, during one of the pauses her weakness obliged her to make in the half incredulous, but wholly indignant comments my explanation had naturally excited.

Her face was already too much flushed to assume a deeper crimson, but her eyes had for a moment an angrier glitter in them as she turned them upon me, and said :—

" You are welcome to the whole truth now, though I recognize no one's right to question or dictate to me. Edmund Hallam wished me to be his wife, and I should probably, but for all you now tell me, have consented to marry him. I did not seek him, Ethel—he sought me. It was not my fault that he was weak and inconstant. Alicia has too little spirit to retain a man's affection. It would have suited me to be the wife of an earl—

you cannot be surprised that, after believing myself what I did, the prospect of a high and honourable position was tempting — too tempting to be resisted. I have suffered, Ethel, far more than your calm English nature can understand, and I did not deserve from Alan the punishment he inflicted on me. I loved him once."

"But now, Meta," I interrupted, speaking as gently as I could, "we must keep to the more essential matter of your present entanglement. Of course you will be content immediately to relinquish whatever claims you may have on Mr. Hallam's affections, which we must hope will return, when he recovers his apparently lost senses, to their rightful owner. You cannot really care for a man you designate as weak and inconstant, and I presume the position of an earl's mother will suit you as well as that of an earl's wife."

"Spare your satire," exclaimed Meta resentfully (I had not intended to be satirical),

" and judge those whose characters resemble your own. I will write to Mr. Hallam to-night, and bid him think of me no more. I do not want to be married now—not I. My boy shall come and live with me and comfort me. Yesterday I should have been glad to know he was dead. To-day I can thank God that he lives, even if he were not to be an earl, and I might have to work for him my life through. Ethel, I am not devoid of human feeling, though you all think I am—all but poor Guy. He loved me; he trusted me; he would cling to me, though the whole bitter world should trample me and my name in the dust. And your mother is kind and tender for his sake. I am grateful to them both."

She was getting so excited and rambling in what she said that I did not think there would be much utility in asking her any question just now, and yet when she thus spoke of Guy the impulse came upon me to say abruptly—

" Meta, why have you misled both Guy and his mother; why especially have you so long permitted him to hope that you might one day acknowledge and repay his devoted love ?"

Her cheeks, which had gradually been growing whiter, flushed a little beneath her sparkling eyes, as she replied distinctly—

" I could not afford to part with the only true, honest affection I was ever likely to have offered to me again. *I will not part with it now*! Guy shall hear all my story from my own lips, and he shall not cease to love me. I repeat it, Ethel—he shall not cease to love me, unworthy though perhaps I am. But first of all I must have my child. I will go for him to-morrow; it would be torture to me to remain here inactive, and pointed at by everybody as the governess sent home in disgrace. Mrs. Vivian liked me in her heart, and would have sympathised with me rather than with Alicia, but for her fear of Edmund's mother. The old lady keeps everybody around her in order; we should have fought desperately had I become her daughter-in-law. The idea of this amused me, for I meant to win her too in the end, and make her forget that she had ever wanted that meek, silent, passionless Alicia for her son's wife. Well, it is all over, as far as I am concerned, now. Alicia will do excellently for a Mrs. Edmund Hallam, to live at Beech-wood, and mind her chickens and her Sunday schools, while my son will inherit the title and estates of the Earl of Clinton, and atone to me for the years of suffering his father doomed me to pass through."

"Meta, you are talking more than is good for you," I said, laying my hand lightly on her arm, and endeavouring not to show how revolted I really was, at much that she had spoken, "You are getting quite feverish, and we shall have to send for a doctor if you don't take care. I think I had better go and fetch you a cup of tea, and then help you into bed. Shall I do so?"

"No, no," she answered impatiently, "I don't want tea, and I cannot go to bed. Have I not that letter to write to Edmund, and my journey of to-morrow to prepare for? But I am very weak, Ethel, from all I have gone through lately, and I should like some wine if you can bring it me. How far is it from here to Devonshire?"

"I believe it will take you a whole day to reach the village where your boy is living," I said, uneasy at her growing restlessness, and anxious to call mamma to see her; "but surely, Meta, you can write, or even send for him. Tired and unwell as you are, it would be folly for you to start upon another journey so soon."

"Folly or not I shall do it," she replied in a determined tone, "I have neglected my child too long, I have shut him out of my heart. I have fought against every soft and tender yearning of which he was the object, because—oh, you know why I have done it, and why I would have persisted in doing it

had the mother's love in me been a thousand-
fold stronger and more passionate than it is.
But the ban is taken off us both—the stigma
is removed. I may hold my innocent child
in my arms and bless him, without fear of
scornful looks or bitter words from married
wives and honorable matrons. And he will
forgive me for leaving him unclaimed till now,
and learn to love me and call me mother! Oh,
Ethel, I think I should be very happy to-day,
if I had a quieter and more tranquilly beating
heart."

She was evidently getting very much exhausted both from the outward fever and the
inward excitement which were uniting to take
away her strength, and would soon, I felt
assured, do her serious mischief if they could
not be subdued.

"Let me fetch you the wine now," I said,
as her eyes closed for a moment and she lay
back on her chair with a little quick gasping
for breath that looked like the approach of an

hysterical fit, " and I think mamma had better come to you."

" As you will," she replied faintly, " only don't let her try to persuade me against going for my boy at once. And, Ethel," as I was turning away, " if Mr. Wyke should be here this evening, ask him to let me have that certificate, and thank him for me, and say that I will see him gladly when I have my child safe in my own keeping, for then we must take immediate steps for establishing his claims, though I will tell all I can in my letter to Edmund to-night. The wine now, please, for I have a strange, sick feeling at my heart, and I must get strength for the work before me."

I fetched my mother as quickly as I could, only giving her, as we went along, a rapid sketch of what had passed, and advising her to compel Meta to remain absolutely quiet for the rest of the evening.

I did not go into the room again myself,

because I knew this was the hour for Gertie to be alone, and I was anxious to have a little sisterly talk with her while we were sure of being uninterrupted.

Mr. Wyke had promised to come to tea, and I was vain enough to think that he would want me all to himself for as long as he could stay at Lindenhurst.

CHAPTER III.

A JOURNEY INTO DEVONSHIRE.

My mother did not succeed a bit better than I had done in calming our guest's excitement, or in persuading her to go to bed. Meta was one of those individuals who, up to a certain point, can (by the force of an imperious will) compel the body to act as a mere " slave of the lamp " to the mind, and who will, to the very last moment of possible endurance, ignore any physical weakness that may threaten to hinder the accomplishment of the purpose on which they have set their heart.

While we were at tea, instead of lying down as she had suffered my mother to believe she intended doing, this very wilful young person contrived to write a long letter to Edmund Hallam, giving him to understand—we will hope somewhat cautiously and tenderly—that he had lost both the inheritance he expected, and the bride he coveted. A very moderate punishment after all, some will say, for his infidelity to his first love, that sweet, gentle Alicia! who had ever been a great deal too good for him, and would now, doubtless, when her wound was healed, find a far worthier object on whom to bestow her affections! Serves Edmund quite right, too, that his retribution should come through Meta, a girl with yellow hair and a warbling voice, who had lured him, as the Syrens lure their victims, to the very brink of destruction. We have no pity, no sympathy, not a grain of charity even to bestow upon a man like this. Let the waves and the billows of affliction and disappointment roll in their fury over him. He deserves whatever he will suffer, and a great deal beyond.

So be it. But if such a judgment went forth from the courts above concerning the very best and most innocent of us all, who might say, who could even contemplate, what our punishment would be?

Mr. Wyke and myself were taking our last turn in the garden—for he had already declared half a dozen times that he must really go—when mamma joined us and told us what Meta had been doing.

"But the letter must not be sent," said the vicar, positively; "until the Earl of Clinton dies I have no authority for bringing that child of Alan Beresford's forward in any way. It was only for Mrs. Beresford's own consolation that I requested Ethel to tell her what her husband confided to me. It is

surely quite possible for this impetuous lady
to decline marrying Mr. Hallam, without
entering into explanations of so very delicate
a nature."

"I am sorry," interrupted my mother, with
a face of grave concern, "that Meta should
not clearly have understood what was exacted
of her in the first instance, for unfortunately
(in her impatience, I should suppose, to undo
some of the mischief she had done) she sent
off her letter while we were at tea. There is
not the slightest hope of our being able to
reclaim it now."

"Then we must just let it rest," said Mr.
Wyke, deeming it useless, I imagine, to express any further annoyance about a misfortune that was without remedy. "Does Mrs.
Beresford still persist in her intention of
travelling into Devonshire to-morrow?"

"Yes," replied mamma, with a sudden and
anxious look towards me, "she is more bent
on it than ever, and when I told her, what

must be indeed very obvious to every one, that she was too ill to undertake such a journey alone, she said she should like to have Ethel with her, but she would have no one else."

Before my mother spoke I had guessed that this was coming, and I had quite satisfied myself that the prospect of attending Meta into Devonshire, and leaving the friend beside me for perhaps three or four days, was as un-pleasing to me as any suddenly suggested plan could well be. But the conviction coming to me at the same time—as it had done on the occasion of mamma's letter recalling either my sister or myself from school—that the thing was settled and inevi-table, I forbore to make any immediate obser-vation, thinking, too, that Mr. Wyke would have something to say about the matter.

At first, however, his hand only sought mine, and held it in a firm, silent pressure, which I understood as meaning that he would not let me go from him without a struggle. This consoled me a little, and I was about to ask mamma what I had better do, when she said again—

"Of course I represented to Meta that you could be ill-spared from home just now, and suggested that perhaps Mrs. Arnott might be glad to accompany her, but she only replied that she was quite prepared to go alone, and would do so if she could not have her cousin Ethel."

"Then I must go," I said, speaking as cheerfully as I could; "there is evidently no help for it."

"It will not be for more than three or four days at the most," added mamma, in a sort of apologetic aside to Mr. Wyke, "and perhaps the change may do her good."

"I think Ethel is very well," he answered, in anything but a consenting voice, and then bending nearer to me, and holding my hand still tighter, he whispered, " my darling! how can I spare you ?"

Mamma left us together to talk it over, and of course I soon talked him into my own conviction that I ought to go—that I must go—that it would be useless, as well as wrong, to fight against a duty so plainly marked out for me.   But he did not like it all ; he shrank —this good man who had suffered so much in the past, and whose whole life was one unselfish devotion to those around him—he shrank from the trifling pain of saying farewell for a few days to a young girl who loved him and esteemed his love a richer treasure than countless worlds could have bestowed upon her.

I think it often happens that great and noble souls bear severe and crushing trials far more heroically than they bear little ones.

Not that this trial seemed a little one just now, either to Mr. Wyke or to me.   Be sure we made the very most of it in our mutual lamentations over its necessity, and said a hundred foolish things about it, and thought it the best possible excuse for prolonging our stroll on the lawn, notwithstanding that we both knew he should have been home an hour ago.

And yet the very terrible and formidable parting was not to come off to-night at all, for the vicar discovered that two ladies could not by any possibility manage to go by themselves to Boltby, and take their own places by the coach, and enquire particulars as to the best way of reaching the obscure village where Meta's boy was to be found. Consequently this kind and obliging friend decided on escorting us thus far, and undertook to order the fly as he went home, and to bring it round for us in the morning.

" For, indeed, I should like," he said, " to shake hands with that poor misguided young creature whose sorrows and whose wrongs interested me once so warmly in her favour,

D 2

and whose relationship to you, my darling, inclines me still to be indulgent to
her many errors.   You will not mind
having me with you as far as Boltby,
Ethel?"

"Yes," I replied, laughing at his lame
excuses for deferring the moment I knew he
dreaded—"I shall mind it very much, Mr.
Wyke—in the way children mind receiving
the choicest gifts from the fairies at Christmas, or on New Year's Day."

Then, without waiting for his acknowledg-
ments (as we had already said good-night
some half-dozen times), I ran off and left
mamma to apologize for my abruptness, and
to expedite his departure.

A pretty hour for an elderly clergyman to
stay out courting! as I had the satisfaction of
overhearing flippant Lizzie Vivian remark
to Fanny Munroe, when, in answer to
the supper bell, they came dancing along
the passage where I stood hidden, while

mamma was closing the front door after the vicar.

     ✿   ✿   ✿   ✿   ✿

"To be loved as you are, Ethel, I would give twenty years of my life, and deem them well bestowed; nay, I think I would die the next hour to enjoy for one hour only the remembrance of such a look directed to me as shone in Mr. Wyke's eyes and made his whole countenance beautiful, when he was bidding you farewell just now. You ought to be happier than any language can express."

Thus spoke Meta as the Devonshire coach which, for the present, we had to ourselves, bowled off the rough Boltby stones on to the smoother road beyond the town, and we could hear each other's voices comfortably. And I, struggling with a foolish, childish inclination to cry beneath my thick veil, replied that I was very happy indeed, and asked if she did not think Mr. Wyke all I had represented him.

For until quite at the last he had addressed his whole conversation to Mrs. Beresford, and she had appeared most grateful for his kindness, warming and brightening under its influence in a manner that was really cheering to see.

"Oh, I do like him excessively," she said, "and am calling myself fool and idiot for having shunned him for so long—shunned the very person, Ethel, who had such glad tidings to give me, and whose friendship, independently of this, would be worth any pains to secure. But it is for your sake he is kind and courteous to me. I do not deceive myself here. You are the very joy and delight of his heart; and you love him dearly, too; you look up to him and honour him as if he wore whiter robes than any other man on earth. So it should be. Love is nothing that is not built on esteem. It fades,

fades, fades, and dies away before the first chill wind, or even a hotter sunbeam than usual that may fall lightly across it. So perished my husband's love for me on his discovery that I was not quite the impossible perfection he had once deemed me."

"Will you tell me something about your married life now, Meta?" I asked, seeing that my companion was in the mood for talking, and feeling that it would be selfish to wrap myself in my own thoughts at such a time.

"There is very little to tell that you have not heard," she answered with a clouding brow. "I loved Alan when he first asked me to marry him, and thought in my ignorance that we might be happy together; I had not learnt enough of my own nature then to fear the result of daily association with the man, who, as an impassioned lover, had satisfied every yearning of my heart. It is surely my misfortune rather than my fault that I have a constant craving for the ardent, romantic love which few husbands, I suppose, ever bestow upon their wives.   Alan was of an exacting, jealous disposition.   He had worshipped a creation of his own which I, his wedded wife, scarcely even imitated.   We were mutually deceived and disappointed; but while his dis-enchantment engendered a morbid, unhealthy despondency that preyed upon his bodily strength, mine only awoke the old yearning for love and sympathy which I found plenty still ready to offer, either in sincerity or to pass away some idle hours.   Ethel, you will not understand what I am telling you though you listen ever so attentively, and though my words shall be as plain and as truthful as any words can be.   A nature like mine could only be understood by a woman who had some answering key notes in her own heart.   You have none, and yet I speak to you, I confide in you as if I were sure both of sympathy and belief."

"Of belief at least you may be sure, Meta," I said encouragingly, as she paused and looked weary of herself and her story, "I know you can have no object in deceiving me."

"At present I certainly have none," she went on a little excitedly, "but I don't know that it is wise to show ourselves quite as we are, even to the most charitable of our friends. And the belief you kindly promise might be harder to yield to me than you can now imagine. So let the past rest for awhile in the darkness to which I had long ago consigned it. There is, I trust, a fairer and a brighter time before me, and I would rather talk with you of that."

"Meta, I would not recal painful memories for the world, to scare away your pleasant thoughts of the future," I said, "but tell me just this, and I will ask no more; your husband was right when he asserted that it was only your love of general admiration, your thirst for universal homage, he had to complain of?"

"No, he was not right," she exclaimed, with a sudden and momentary fierceness that quite startled me, "neither would you be right in the conclusion you would naturally draw from this avowal of mine." Then, relapsing into her ordinary manner, she added coldly:

"There is no medium in the understandings of most people between a vulgar craving for the admiration of the multitude—such a craving as your pretty Graybourne widow acknowledges and manifests—and that other thing which I, as much as you, pure English girl! should shrink from naming. I wanted affection, tenderness, heart homage when I was a wife, as I had wanted them before. My husband thought when I was seeking these I was seeking the common admiration which every decent looking grisette or barmaid can inspire. I wronged him, Ethel, I grant you, but he wronged me more, and I can feel no remorse, no repentance, as far as he is concerned. Another time, if you are really interested in looking closer into a nature that is still a puzzle as well as a torment to itself, I will make you my confessor. Now it gives me the horrors to recal that weary past at all. Won't you enliven me by talking of Mr. Wyke, and your own untroubled courtship?"

I scarcely know why this sudden request of my cousin's should have had the effect of showing me more clearly than anything that had yet passed, the great gulf that lay between her and me. But so it was. I felt that not for worlds could I have unveiled my heart for her inspection, or yielded to her curious and perhaps amused observation the heart of the friend whose dignity I valued even more than my own.

The way in which Meta could speak of her dead husband; her apparent forgetfulness or recklessness of the misery she might have created in the Hallam family; her wholly selfish anticipations in reference to the future —all these things had struck me comparatively little as they were successively brought before me—but now when she asked me lightly to talk to her of Mr. Wyke and of those treasured looks and words which I held sacred even from my own dear sister, I was conscious of a sudden shrinking, that might have fallen short of perfect charity, from this cousin of mine; and I answered her with an involuntary coldness that sealed her lips for awhile, and made me welcome the entrance, from a road side inn, of a male passenger who was sufficiently young and good looking (though probably not above the rank of a farmer) to engage Meta's attention if she still felt disposed for conversation.

It was at least half an hour, however, before this new comer took the slightest notice of either of us. He was reading a county paper that seemed to interest him immensely, to judge by the very complacent expression of his countenance, and the occasional snaps of the fingers in which, heedless of our presence, he indulged.

At length, when he had gone through the four large, close pages a second time, he yawned, stretched himself, and finally glancing across at Meta, said politely—

"Like to see the paper, Miss?"

"Is there any news in it?" my cousin asked languidly; for by this time some of her artificial strength was beginning to give way, and her face exhibited signs of much weariness and exhaustion.

"Plenty of news," the young man replied briskly—"though perhaps not the sort of news you ladies care for. There's a good deal about the crops and the farming interest generally, and there's a long account of the meeting of Sir Harry Vaux's hounds on Friday, and there's a lot of births, deaths, and marriages, with an earl's death amongst them.

Perhaps" (handing over the paper), "you would like to look for yourself, Miss."

Eagerly Meta availed herself of his courtesy now, and quickly and with a flushing cheek her eye ran over the columns of the paper till she came to something that arrested her at once, and made her read as if her heart as well as her eyes had a sudden power of vision.

In five minutes she looked up, trembling and white now, from excitement. I gave her a smelling bottle I had in my bag, and then took the paper (our companion was luckily asleep by this time), and read the following:

" THE LATE EARL OF CLINTON. We regret to state that this aged nobleman expired last evening, after a tedious illness, at his mansion in Grosvenor Square. We understand that in default of natural heirs (the Earl never having married), the title and estates descend to a Mr. Hallam, through his mother, who is nearly connected with the illustrious family in ques-

tion. Clinton Park, in Hertfordshire, is said
to be one of the finest country seats in England, and the whole estate attached to the
earldom is computed at about forty-five
thousand a year. Further particulars will be
given in our next number."

"Poor Edmund Hallam!" was my first
instinctive exclamation, as I laid down the
paper and looked up at my pale *vis-à-vis*.
"He will get your letter, Meta, about the same
time that this news will reach him."

"And my boy is now the Earl of Clinton!"
she replied, drawing a long breath, and seeming to have no room in her mind for any
thought but this. "Ethel, I shall take him
to Clinton Park at once—you must come with
us, and I shall invite Guy—and—"

"Thank you," I interrupted, hardly able
to suppress my indignation; "but I could
in no case do that, Meta, as I am now giving
up to you time that is claimed elsewhere. But
you forget that your child's right will have to

be established legally, before you can take possession of his inheritance. It is scarcely likely that the Hallams will abandon their claims upon your bare word, or even upon Mr. Wyke's when he confirms what you have stated. It may be months and months before the matter is finally decided."

" That will be detestably vexatious," said Meta, who in those few minutes had doubtless constituted herself mistress of Clinton Park and all its belongings—" but of course I shall have the first legal advisers that are to be obtained, and they will advance me any money I may require. My little Alan, my small earl in frocks and baby shoes, must at once be supplied with the state and luxuries befitting his rank. Oh, Ethel, I wish I could get my weak body to sympathize more than it does with the gladness and lightness of my mind. I am sick and faint and weary, when I ought to have the strength of a lioness who is returning to her long lost young. Give me some of the medicine you brought for me, and let me try to sleep."

As it was very clear that she would work herself into a fever, if sleep did not come, I gave her a pretty strong dose of a powerful soporific mamma had put up to be used in case of need, when Meta went to bed after her journey.

This soon produced the desired effect, and both for her own health's sake and because the chasm between us seemed to be opening even wider and wider, I rejoiced unfeignedly in the temporary leave to commune with my own thoughts which I thus secured. The young man slept too, till, late in the afternoon, the coach stopped at the place it was bound for, a market town of some importance in South Devonshire, and from whence we should have to proceed by any conveyance we could get to the village—about twelve or thirteen miles distant—where Meta's child resided.

Of course I was obliged to rouse my cousin

now, but her long rest had done her good, and she was able to make a tolerable meal with me in the little inn parlour, to which we thankfully betook ourselves, as soon as we left the coach.

This over, we rang and enquired whether we could have a carriage of any kind to convey us at once to the small hamlet—Yardley by name—that we desired especially to reach that night.

"Yardley, Yardley," repeated the landlady, who had answered our summons in person, "well, for sure, that's the place where they do say they've had the scarlet fever awful these last few weeks. You'll not be going to make any long stay there, ladies, I hope."

"I think not," quickly replied Meta, whose wholly preoccupied mind evidently associated no alarming ideas with this intelligence, "but I have a little boy staying there, and what you tell us makes it only the more imperative that I should fetch him away as soon as possible. Can we have a carriage in half an hour?"

" Certainly—that is, I think so," said the woman, bustling out of the room, but not before I had noticed a strange, pitying look come into her honest face, as if she could understand why a parent with a child at Yardley should be in a hurry to get to him.

Fortunately for Meta, though she was that parent, she saw nothing but the dazzling visions her imagination was presenting to her of future triumphs and honours for the mother and guardian of the young Earl of Clinton.

CHAPTER IV.

ALAN, EARL OF CLINTON.

THEY were lovely scenes we were passing through; and enjoying them intensely myself, thinking the waving corn fields, the deep wooded coombes, the far off hills, blue and shadowy in the distance, objects worth noticing and talking about, I noticed them and talked of them to my silent companion, judging that it would be best for her in every way to have her mind diverted, even temporarily,

from the one object that was so entirely en-
grossing it.

But Meta, though professing to be an
ardent lover of nature, and having really, I
believe, a kind of artistic appreciation of it,
was not to-night in a mood for listening to or
sympathising with my raptures.

As we approached nearer to our destination
her very unusual taciturnity increased. I
could not get a single word, good or bad,
from her, till, following out some rather
anxious thoughts of my own which had been
growing since we left the inn, I said, suddenly:

"Meta, didn't it give you quite a turn when
that woman told us about the scarlet fever
having been so bad at Yardley? It did me, I
know, though I was afraid to say so to you
at the time. Children are so very apt to take
any infectious malady of this kind."

She scarcely allowed me time to finish this
last observation before she turned, and almost
glared at me, in her wrathful indignation.

" Ethel, you would drive a weaker woman than myself mad with your absurd fears and suggestions. I suppose, if two people in the village have had a fever within a twelvemonth, it would be sufficient to set afloat such a report as we have heard. Yardley is a particularly healthy place, I know, for when Mr. Beresford sent away my child, and I asked him what he had done with it, he said it was gone to be brought up in a beautiful English village, where the air was so pure and good that the boy *must* grow strong and well. But even if the scarlet fever was at Yardley, why should my Alan have it?"

I felt inclined to say, " Why should he not, as well as others?" but seeing how irritable my former observation had made my cousin, I only replied quietly—

" I did not intend to vex you, Meta. I spoke out what I had been thinking of—that was all. Shall I ask the driver how far we are now from Yardley?"

" As you please. I am excessively tired, and shall be glad to have done with travelling for to-day at least. If the old ladies cannot give us a bed, we shall, of course, find accommodation in the village."

She seemed as eager to talk now as she had been to keep silence before, by which I guessed that my words had awakened some degree of unacknowledged anxiety in her.

In reply to my enquiry, the driver informed us that we were just mounting the hill, at the bottom of which the village of Yardley was situated; "you'll be seeing it presently, ladies," he added, "and I hope you won't have had too much of it before you gets away again. If all's true as folks around us have been saying, the grave diggers have had a fine time of it there lately: but one or another of these low-lying villages mostly gets a bad fever every two or three years."

I looked stealthily at Meta as the man spoke, and thought I observed that she grew paler at this new testimony concerning the Yardley epidemic; but she did not utter a word expressive of any particular emotion, and I felt reluctant to do more than I had already done in awakening fears that might be altogether groundless.

We desired the driver, as we at length entered the long narrow street of the village, to enquire at the post office the way to Salem Cottage, the residence of the Misses Beresford. We were told it stood quite out of Yardley on the other side, and this information, while it brought some relief to my own mind, evidently lulled all Meta's fears, and raised her spirits to the same buoyant level they had reached in the early part of the day, when she had first read the announcement of the old Earl's death.

" Please, sir, that be Salem Cottage," said a ragged urchin who was throwing pebbles into a pool of water by the road side, in answer to another enquiry on the part of our driver—" that little white house with the hill agin it, and the big cedar in front.   The lane's a'most too narrow for carriages to get up."

" Then we will descend at once," exclaimed Meta, jumping up, and opening the carriage door herself in her very natural impatience.

" Ethel, you will be kind enough to settle with the man, while I walk on to the cottage. This boy will bring our travelling bags up for us."

Which, in consideration of a fourpenny piece, the youth in question joyfully consented to do, and both he and Meta were half way up the deeply rutted lane before I was ready to follow them.

When I reached my cousin she was standing almost breathless before the low, white gate, which led into the pretty front garden of Salem cottage, and had just rung the bell (she told me) loudly, for the second time.   I paid the boy, took the bags from him, and sent him away. As yet I had discovered nothing to indicate that Alan, Earl of Clinton, had suffered from his vicinage to the fever-haunted locality. The blinds of the house were not drawn closer or lower than the warmth of the day seemed to render necessary, and under the cedar tree stood a painted wooden horse on wheels—a child's toy that might have been left there when the young earl was called in to his tea an hour or two ago. I pointed this out to Meta, who smiled and said rather loftily—

" Dear boy ! he shall have richer playthings than that for the time to come—something that will better match the coronet that has descended upon him."

As she spoke, a female of very demure and grave aspect came slowly down the pathway from the house, looking at us as she approached the gate neither very kindly nor unsuspiciously.

" We want to see the Miss Beresfords at once," said Meta, a little imperiously. "We have already rung the bell twice, and waited a long time here. Are they not at home?"

" They are at home," the woman answered, all unmoved by my cousin's rebuke—"but you are strangers, and I am quite sure they cannot see you. They would not see their dearest friends if they chanced to call to-day. We have death in the house!"

There was something in the inexpressibly calm way in which the prim, quaker-like woman uttered these words, that struck a deeper sense of awe and solemnity into my heart than the same words, spoken in the most tragic and impassioned voice, would have done. For one moment I was literally so stunned by it that I forgot to think of Meta, and was only recalled by hearing her say, with apparent composure, though the words came out quickly with a sort of jerk ; " What death ? whose ? tell me instantly. I have a right to ask."

" Right or no right, ma'am," responded the woman, now for the first time looking, I fancied, somewhat curiously at Meta, " I can have no objection to answering your question.

It is a poor little boy that my mistresses generously adopted and were bringing up as their own, that is lying dead in the house at this moment. He took the fever a week ago, and was doing as well as could be till yesterday evening, when quite sudden like, the symptoms changed, and he was dead before morning."

I turned round instinctively, sick and faint as I felt myself, to put my arm round poor Meta ; but she thrust me from her with some passionate exclamation that I did not understand, and forcing open the gate, which had not been locked, rushed, like a thing possessed, up the path to the cottage.

I was going to follow her, when the woman who had for a minute watched the flying figure, stood straight before me, and said in a low voice, as if afraid her words might be heard even by the wind :

"Is it his mother ?"

"Yes, yes," I cried impatiently ; "but do

let me get to her. Poor girl! she will go mad."

I paid no heed to the groaning that succeeded my acknowledgment of Meta's relationship to the dead child, but finding the way clear for me, ran swiftly up the path my cousin had taken, and in through the open door of the cottage where she stood, white, speechless, and with wild eyes, confronting a very small elderly lady with a face disfigured by crying, and a look that was half fear, half amazement, directed towards her incomprehensible guest.

"She was his mother," I faltered out, as Miss Beresford on my arrival turned her attention with manifest relief to me, "she came to claim and take him away with her. We only heard from your servant—of—of—"

I could not get out the word for my own emotion which was choking me, and now there appeared another small old lady on the scene, whose face was also disfigured by crying, and whose hands the first grasped eagerly, as she said, with such an odd, shocked expression coming with an increase of red into her countenance :

" Alan's mother, Naomi—what shall we do with her ? "

It was not until the second sister had flushed deeply too, and retired instinctively a few paces from where Meta stood, that it suddenly occurred to me to remember the error they were under.   I said immediately, though not without a feeling of indignation against what seemed a pharisaical spirit in these quaint old gentlewomen :

" My cousin—Mrs. Beresford—came also to announce the death of the Earl of Clinton and the succession of her son to the title and estate.   The late Mr. Alan Beresford left ample proofs of his lawful marriage to this lady, who is, I fear, in urgent need of some present care and tenderness from all of us. The shock has been so very great."

Then both the sisters (whose momentary shrinking from a woman they believed impure had been more the result of a life-long habit of thought and principle, than any lack of christian charity), advanced to the poor, stricken mother, and led her, unresistingly now, to a little dainty room on the side of the hall, where they placed her tenderly on a soft couch, and looked at me to know what could next be done for her.

Alas! I could not tell. This was not like any common illness. Meta appeared to have lost suddenly the power of speech, while the agonized expression in the large dilated eyes, indicated that the mind had all its activity and all its capacity of suffering still left to it.

Quiet for the present I, at length, suggested, and a doctor as soon as one could be obtained. There was nothing else that I could think of, unless Meta could herself give us, even by signs, any idea of what might benefit or relieve her.

" You ask her, Naomi," said the youngest
Miss Beresford, with an appealing glance towards her sister, who, I concluded, was the
strongest minded of the two. " It makes me
quiver all over to look at the poor thing."

Whereupon the eldest of the small old
ladies knelt down by the sofa where they had
placed Meta, and in a very sweet, compas-
sionate voice, asked her if there was anything
in the world they could do for her.

No answer, no sign that the words were
even heard with the outward ear; only that
wild, anguished look in the fixed eyes with
which she had first confronted the meek
spinster who had opened the door to her.

" Send down Judith to the village for Dr.
Lloyd at once," said the eldest Miss Beresford
to her sister, " and take this other lady up
stairs, while I remain here with our poor
nephew's wife. We have a nice cheerful room
we can offer you."

This last observation was addressed to me,

and having thanked the kind speaker and told her how gratefully I accepted her hospitality both for myself and my cousin, I followed the second sister from the little parlour, and stood by while she gave her hurried and scarcely intelligible order to the prim Judith.

" Does the young person seem very ill, ma'am ?" this respectable, middle-aged damsel ventured to ask of her mistress, with some kindly interest in her voice, notwithstanding her evident impression that Meta was a " young person " who ought to be beyond the pale of human sympathies.

" The lady in the parlour is exceedingly ill, Judith," replied Miss Beresford, with sudden dignity, though again the red glowed brighter on her grief stained cheek; "and as you will be asked questions I may tell you at once that our guest is Mrs. Beresford, the mother of the dear child who has gone to his eternal home, and the wife of our late nephew. This lady is Mrs. Beresford's cousin, and we desire that they may both receive every possible care and attention for as long as they honour us by remaining under our roof."

If for a moment it struck me that this explanation was an unnecessary concession to the prejudices of an ignorant and uncharitable woman, whose narrow mind would see contamination to itself in the very shadow of a fallen sister darkening the threshold of a virtuous dwelling, I thought otherwise when I observed the effect of Miss Beresford's words upon the individual to whom they were addressed.

The cold and rather forbidding countenance unbent as under a sense of positive relief; the lines of the face grew softer and more woman-like; a briskness and energy seemed to come at an inward summons into the whole aspect, and even the voice partook of the favourable change, as Judith answered eagerly:

"I won't be gone ten minutes, ma'am, and I'll sit up all night with the poor dear lady, and I'll run my legs off and be glad too if I can be of any use to her. Oh, dear, oh dear, what a wonderful world we do live in, and how good the Lord is to make things straight to us when they've long been crooked, or we have thought them so."

"That is a most valuable and faithful servant," said Miss Beresford, as she helped me to unpack our travelling bags, and waited while I brushed and arranged my dusty apparel; "but she has her peculiar crotchets, and not all the lecturing in the world would ever beat them out of her. She never quite forgave our adoption of our poor little darling, because we could offer no satisfactory account of his parentage. Her own evident love for the child she regarded as a sin to be struggled against; and though I believe she grieves for his death only less than we do, she has never, in our presence, shed a tear, but worn, ever since he died, that cold, repellant aspect, which seemed meant to rebuke our sorrow by reminding us that a child of shame was better in Heaven than on earth."

"And you believe her." I said, "to be a good woman for all this?"

"I know her to be an admirable, unselfish, devoted creature," replied the dear little woman, warmly; "and you will see that now the mystery which perplexed her is cleared up, she will display the zeal and the kindness of ten ordinary women in ministering to that poor young mother, whose story I should like to hear by and bye."

"Not from me," I silently determined, for I could say so little good of my unhappy cousin, and at such a moment I should have felt myself a wretch in saying anything bad.

As I turned from the completion of my hurried toilet to ask my companion if we had not better go down to her sister and Meta, she said in a suppressed voice, and with tears rushing to her eyes :

"You would like to see our darling? Come with me."

I had been already far too much excited and agitated to have the least wish to go through another trying scene, but as my assent to the proposition was assumed as a matter of course, I followed my conductress, without a word, to the chamber of the dead.

He lay in his little shroud on a large, old-fashioned four-post bed, in the centre of a half-darkened room—a fair, slight child, with soft yellow hair like his mother's. Very pretty he must have been in life and health; very pure and calm and angelic he looked in that long, last sleep, into which he had so early fallen. A white lily, emblem of his yet uncorrupted innocence, had been placed in one of the small, fair hands, while other flowers were strewn around his pillow, and over the snowy coverlet of the bed.

And this was all that remained to the poor, proud, rebellious-hearted mother,—of Alan, Earl of Clinton!

CHAPTER V.

NEIGHBOURLY CONGRATULATIONS.

THE village doctor, who could ill spare the time for a new patient, made three visits to the cottage before he could decide on the exact nature of Meta's strange seizure. Something approaching to catalepsy he inclined at first to consider it, and something approaching to catalepsy he still called it when, on the evening of the second day, her power of speech returned to her, and floods and floods —ever increasing—of passionate tears, while they relieved the long pressure on the brain, left her too utterly weak and exhausted for the sleep she so much needed not to come to her.

During all this time the attention and care she received from the good old ladies and the now untiring and devoted Judith, were things beyond my powers of describing. To them this living object to think and work for, at a moment when their hearts were well nigh breaking over the death of the child they had adopted and passionately loved, was really a Godsend, and one for which I am sure, in their inmost souls, they were deeply thankful. Finding me indisposed to enter at any length on the circumstances of Meta's past life, they soon ceased asking questions, content, now they knew she had been married to their nephew, to accept her on trust, and to give her credit for every virtue the owner of so fair a face, and their lost darling's mother, ought surely to possess.

I am quite positive it never once occurred

to these single-hearted, innocent old ladies, that Meta's wild regret at the child's death was in any way connected with the honours he had missed, and that she—his mother—would miss through him. And as for her long, voluntary relinquishment of all claims upon her son, they were disposed to regard this, not only with indulgence, but with favour, when I told them the impression under which her husband had left her concerning the illegality of their marriage.

"For of course, poor young thing!" they innocently observed; "her very heart must have yearned for re-union to the precious child, and it could only have been a most natural feeling of self-respect and modesty which kept her from seeking him. Alan Beresford was ever a strange, fanciful, morbid creature, and no doubt he greatly exaggerated in his own mind, as well as to us, the weaknesses and short-comings of this hapless Meta."

So, seeing into what good, kind hands this hapless Meta had at length fallen, I announced in my letter home, the second evening, that, unless she was worse the next morning, I should return to Lindenhurst that day. The Miss Beresfords had wished me to remain till after the funeral, but I told them frankly how I was situated, and they forbore to urge the matter.

The sleep which exhaustion had procured for my cousin, doubtless saved both her life and her reason—so at least the doctor asserted—but we were all surprised and disappointed when, on her awaking in the morning, she seemed so very little better in any way.

Whether she really knew those around her or not, I did not feel competent to decide. Nobody except myself, however, had the slightest doubt on the subject, for she appeared quite unconscious still, and her words, when she spoke, were in her own language, and consequently unintelligible to any of her hearers. Mr. Lloyd was of opinion that the brain was not entirely relieved of its pressure yet, but said that it would be all right by and bye if her bodily strength could be kept up by stimulants.

This for the present was the great difficulty that we had to overcome, for the throat was closed (by hysterià), as effectually as it would have been had a real physical obstruction suddenly formed itself there. Under these circumstances, I felt it right to wait another day at Yardley, and towards evening there was a manifest improvement in our patient—she had swallowed a few spoonfuls of brandy and a little beef-tea. Dr. Lloyd looked cheerful when he came, and said she would now do well.

So in the morning, very early, I bade the kind old ladies good-bye, left a note to be given to my cousin as soon as she was in a condition to read it, and started gladly and thankfully on my homeward journey.

It was late in the afternoon when I arrived at Boltby, not too tired to forget that I had been tired at all, when I saw Mr. Wyke standing at the coach office to receive me, and knew by his look, even before he could speak a word of welcome, how I had been missed and longed for.

" My darling, you must never leave me again! " he said, as, in accordance with my wish, we commenced our homeward walk through the fields; " I can do without a great many things, but I cannot do without you, Ethel, my love, my child, my wife ! "

And I, quite as happy and joyous as he was at this reunion, declared emphatically that I would never, never leave him again of my own free will.   Did he not believe me?

" My dearest," he answered fondly, " if I did not believe you, I fear, however much I might desire it otherwise for duty's sake, the burden of life would become too heavy for me."

Then I repeated my assertion again with additional earnestness, and no warning voice whispered to me that, in my shortsightedness and folly, I was promising what I should fail to perform.

After I had told with a minuteness that my letter had been unable to convey everything that there was to tell about Meta, and we had for a short time discussed her strange destiny, I asked eagerly for home news, and first of all about our dear Maggie.

She was about the same, the father said, certainly not worse, but longing to have me with her again, and forming all sorts of plans for the sea-side where her new mamma would begin to live with her altogether.

" And you must really make haste with your preparations, Ethel," added this unreasonable vicar, " because the autumn is getting on rapidly, and by-and-bye it will be too cold to take Maggie away at all. I cannot give you above three weeks at farthest."

" Very well," I replied, laughing; " then you and Mr. Kenyon, and any other gentleman you may know, must buy thimbles, and come and help to make my new dresses, for I am sure there are not enough women folk in Graybourne to get me ready in the time."

" Nonsense," he said, a little gravely, for I believe he thought I meant it; " a clergyman's wife, Ethel, requires scarcely any finery, and none except the wedding dress that cannot be made as well after as before the marriage. I shall take off a week now, and only allow you a fortnight."

" And I shall turn you over altogether to mamma for this discussion," I replied; " and forbid your ever naming it to me again. Have you seen Gertie since I have been from home ?"

" Yes ; I walked to Lindenhurst with

Walter the evening after you left. We were both asked to stay to tea, and your sister was very gracious and pleasant. I did not think her looking well. By the bye, there have been long letters from Cambridge, I understand, in which you are mainly concerned. Your mother is waiting your return to write Guy some account of Mrs. Beresford's proceedings."

"I cannot endure," I said—"to think of Guy now in connection with Meta. Her misfortunes will endear her all the more to him, and there is nothing but his poverty can save him from becoming her husband."

"But that probably will do it," Mr. Wyke replied cheeringly—"so don't run into your usual mistake, Ethel, of meeting troubles half way. I have not told you yet that I wrote to the Hallams on seeing the announcement of the old earl's death, confirming what your cousin had previously disclosed to Edmund. Two days later I sent off the intelligence of the child's death. I am rather surprised that no notice was taken of my first letter."

"It seems a pity, as things have turned out, that they ever heard a word about Alan Beresford's son. I hope that neither this nor Meta's conduct will have occasioned much distress in the family."

"We must wait and see," remarked the good vicar thoughtfully; and then we talked of other things till we reached Lindenhurst, where my fatigue became too manifest to be any longer concealed, and I was glad to rest on the sofa and let the others talk for the remainder of the evening.

How the next fortnight went by I scarcely know. What between visits to Maggie, long walks with her father (who because I had a good deal of sitting on behalf of that formidable needlework declared that I needed additional air and exercise), the work itself, and the frequent calls of our kind neighbours, I never had a single moment for calm reflection, and my brain was fast getting into a state of hopeless confusion.

During this time we had tolerably good accounts of Meta, who was progressing very slowly, but on the whole, Miss Beresford wrote, " quite as well as could be expected, poor dear !" She had never expressed a wish to see her boy, although her mind had fully regained its clearness before the funeral took place, and the sisters both thought it "just a little strange " that since then she had asked so few questions about her lost darling, and evinced so very small an interest in the details they were never weary of repeating to her concerning all he had said and done during the four years they had been happy enough to have the charge of him.

To me this fact appeared much less strange than it had done to the Miss Beresfords ; but I was glad that Meta had found such kind and indulgently disposed relatives, and I hoped with all my heart that, even when she got quite well and strong again, they would prevail on her to continue amongst them.

A few days after my return home Mr. Wyke was summoned very unexpectedly one morning to Beechwood. Mrs. Hallam had arrived there the night before, and was most anxious to see him.

Alicia Clarkson, or what, he said, he might reasonably have mistaken for her ghost, received him in the drawing room, and told him the lady of the house would be down presently. They were in great trouble, the poor girl added, on account of Edmund's mysterious disappearance, and the failure of all the means they had hitherto employed to gain tidings of him. On Mr. Wyke's further questioning, she admitted that a letter he had received from Mrs. Beresford (Alicia gave Meta her proper name) was supposed to be the cause of his flight from his mother and herself. Prior to this, Alicia herself had suspected that he had ceased to care for her,

and that he was engaged in a very serious
flirtation with Meta; but up to the time of
his leaving home, Mrs. Hallam had never
acknowledged to any similar suspicion. He
had read to them both that part of the letter
which related to the existence of Alan Beresford's child, and the consequent loss to
Edmund of his long expected inheritance.
They thought he seemed unnaturally excited,
as he had never been an ambitious man, and
the earldom, as far as they knew, had always
appeared to be a matter of little moment to
him. But that same evening he had dis-
appeared, leaving only a couple of lines
addressed to his mother, bidding her have no
anxiety about him and entreating her not
to seek him, as he felt himself unworthy both
of her love and the love of the girl he had
once hoped to marry, but whom he now re-
leased absolutely from all vows and promises
of which he had been the object.

But in spite of the off-hand manner in

which Mrs. Hallam chose to speak of her son's self banishment, Mr. Wyke felt assured that it was, in reality, affecting her deeply, and that, putting the earldom aside, she would give a great deal to have him safe at home again. The vicar could only advise her to persevere with the advertisements she had already caused to be inserted in all the English and foreign journals of any importance, and, while waiting their result, to appoint a trustworthy agent to manage the estate. He also suggested that both Alicia and herself should take a journey to Clinton Park, as the change would do them good, and she might, as Edmund's mother, be able at least to begin remedying much that had gone wrong in consequence of the late earl's neglect.

The old lady said she would take this matter into consideration, but they had been a long while absent from Beechwood, and she had no inclination at all to move again.

" And then, Ethel," said Mr. Wyke, when he had repeated all the above to me after his visit to Beechwood, " I had something in my turn to communicate, something which Mrs. Hallam expressed herself very pleased to hear, adding that a man could not go very far wrong in selecting either of good Mr. Beamish's daughters for a wife. But you will hear more from the old lady's own lips, as she intends to call upon you and present her wedding gift in person."

Which she did, not many days after the vicar had seen her; nearly overwhelming me with the warmth and graciousness of her congratulations, and hanging round my neck a most exquisite little watch and chain which she said the wife of a clergyman, who did her duty, would find useful as well as ornamental. In the midst of my earnest thanks and blushes she cut me short by the unexpected observation, half spoken to herself I imagine:

" It only surprises me that the vicar did

not take the eldest and the handsomest sister, for even saints are but mortal men while upon earth; but I suppose he knows best what he is about—and now good-bye, my dear, for I have left Alicia at home with a frightful headache, and I told her I should not be away long."

The widow from Primrose Cottage came, amongst the rest, to felicitate me upon my happy prospects, and to apologize for the great mistake she had made in reference to Miss Dora.

" But it was too bad of you not to set me right at the time, fair lady," she added in a little tone of pique, " for I cannot believe that you had not, even then, a very good notion of how the land really lay. As for me, I only repeated what I had heard from others, and how could it ever have occurred to me that a man of Mr. Wyke's age would choose a girl like you ? Of course I am not surprised at him—but you—well, I suppose you recollected the ancient adage, 'better be an old man's darling' &c., &c. I daresay you will get on charmingly together."

The arrow did not even prick my outer skin. I smiled and told her I felt sure of getting on well with so good and admirable a man, whose preference had raised me to a height I had never ventured to contemplate before. If Mr. Wyke was satisfied with me, I was more than satisfied with him. I felt not less honored than happy in the prospect of becoming his wife.

Upon which Mrs. Arnott screwed up her mouth, and made a little bow expressive of her sense of my rebuke, but in another minute she was rattling on again as flippantly as ever, advising me to take advantage of my youth to gain an influence over my elderly husband, declaring that the only pleasure in life· was having one's own way, and ruling the proud animals who called themselves lords of the creation.

"There is," she said, "but one thing I have ever been able to admire or understand in all Tennyson's poetry that people make such a fuss about, and that is what Cleopatra grandly asserts in ' the dream of fair women.'

> " ' There are no men to govern in this wood ;
> That makes my only woe !'

"Isn't it beautifully natural, Miss Ethel? I am sure you are struck with it, and you will adopt my advice about getting at your husband's blind side. Bless you! if *I* was going to marry an old man, wouldn't I lead him a pretty dance? I wonder how your vicar would have liked me for a wife."

When I repeated to Mr. Wyke, with a view of amusing him, the substance of this pleasant lady's conversation, and wound up by asking him how he would have liked her for a helpmate, he looked so aghast, and shuddered so violently, that I was not surprised at his saying :

" Ethel, don't jest on the subject of my antipathy to Mrs. Arnott. I have told you before how real it is, and though it may be incomprehensible to you, I hope you will henceforth both remember and respect it."

From this time, however often the little widow dropped in to see how the dresses were getting on, and indulge in her passion for chit-chat, I never troubled the vicar with an account of her visits; and I have reason to think that he was grateful for my forbearance.

It had been arranged between mamma and myself, Gertie also approving, that as Guy was to come home to my wedding to give me away in the place of our lost father, it would be best to defer telling him anything about Meta until he was with us. Her story had not as yet got circulated abroad, and the little that the Graybourne people (with the exception of the family at Beechwood) knew or guessed of it, would not be likely to penetrate as far as Cambridge.

Just two evenings before the wedding, which we had managed—continually urged on by the vicar—to be ready for in little more than the fortnight, as it was growing dark, and mamma, on Mr. Wyke's departure, had called me into her room to have a nice quiet talk with her, the Beechwood carriage suddenly drew up before our gates, and Alicia Clarkson, whom I had not yet seen, descended alone from it.

"Poor girl!" said my mother, feelingly; "she has doubtless only come to see you, Ethel, and will be glad to escape a meeting with the rest of us. Run down and take her into the drawing-room, and I will manage that no one shall intrude upon you while she is with you."

And "poor girl!" was in my heart, if not on my lips, as dear Alicia put her little thin hand into mine, and, striving hard to speak cheerfully and bravely, wished me joy.

"I could not come sooner," she said, when

we were safely shut in the room to which I had led her, and seated side by side on the sofa. "I have not been very well, Ethel; but I have thought of you continually, and been so glad of your happiness. Mr. Wyke is a man you can trust—a good christian man—and loving you once he will love you always. I have brought you only a little ring, Ethel, which I should be pleased if you would wear for my sake."

She looked so ethereal, so spirit-like as she spoke, that her words seemed to me quite sad and ominous. I knew the tears were in my eyes as I kissed her fondly, and told her the ring should never leave my finger again. Then I said:

"Dear Alicia, you are not very ill, are you? —nobody thinks there is anything serious the matter with you, do they?"

"I don't know," she replied, wearily; "I don't think so myself, because it seems to me that it would be too much happiness to die and be at rest; but this is a wrong, rebellious feeling, and I try to struggle against it. If I only could be sure that he was alive and well, I think I could grow more patient and submissive. It is this cruel suspense that kills me."

" Alicia," I said, "tell me one thing. Could you forgive Edmund and receive him into your heart again if he came home penitent, and anxious to atone for the wrong he has done ?"

Her lovely face was crimson dyed, as she answered meekly :

" My heart has never cast him out for one moment, Ethel. Do you remember the conversation you and I had months ago about the possibility of loving on when esteem had ceased. I said I thought it would be possible, but very, very terrible. So I find it, and yet not for worlds would I give up this love if I might. Dear Ethel, I did not come here to be egotistical or sentimental," she added, in a suddenly changed tone. " Forgive me, and take one more assurance of my earnest rejoicing in your happiness. We start to-morrow for Clinton Park. When I see you again you will be no longer my friend, Ethel Beamish."

"But your friend always, dearest Alicia," I said, embracing her tenderly, and feeling as if her sadness and desolation rebuked my own exceeding peace and contentment—" and who knows what bright, sunshiny days may be in store for you yet!"

She only shook her head, without again trusting her voice to utter a word, and ran swiftly down to the carriage that was waiting for her.

The day following this, Guy arrived at home.

CHAPTER VI.

MARRIED.

WE all felt that it would be far better if possible to defer any lengthy explanations to Guy on the subject of Meta, until after my wedding, but we had little hope—mamma, I am sure, none—of being able to put him off with less than the entire story. And we judged him only too correctly; for the moment he had kissed us all, and held me a little longer than the others in his affectionate embrace, telling me that I was the luckiest girl in the whole world he sat down amongst us, and without giving even his mother time to comment upon his improved appearance and increased manliness, exclaimed, impulsively and eagerly—

"Now then, I want to hear at once everything you have to tell about Meta. She has not written to me for the last two months, and all of you in your letters have politely ignored the numerous and repeated questions I have put to you concerning her."

So there was clearly no help for it; and Gertie and myself, on a preconcerted signal, slipped quietly out of the room, leaving to mamma the unenviable task of narrating, to this infatuated lover of Meta, the long, sad story of her errors, and her wrongs.

It was then about six o'clock in the evening, and we did not meet our brother again until supper time, when I noticed that he looked very pale and excited, and would eat nothing that was offered to him. My mother's mild countenance expressed both grief and a little apprehension, and I don't believe her eyes were ever for two minutes together removed from Guy's face.

As this was my last evening at home, I did not feel in a very calm state of mind myself, and as soon as supper was over I got up, and, pointing to the moonlight streaming through our window, invited my sister to a turn with me in the garden. Her pupils had left her the day before for the Michaelmas holidays—Lizzie Vivian to join her family for a week or two at Brighton, and the little Munroes to stay the same time with some friends, who had come unexpectedly to reside about fifteen miles from Graybourne. So Gertie, having lost her occupation for awhile, was dull and out of spirits, and twice that day I had caught her with Walter's green book upon her lap, and her eyes, having unmistakeable tears in them, fixed upon nothing that other eyes could discern.

She rose with apparent willingness when I proposed taking her with me into the garden, and as we passed Guy I bent to kiss the back of his curly head, and to whisper an entreaty that he would come out to us presently also. He made no reply, which hurt me for the moment, till I recollected what wholly absorbing things love and its interests become to some natures, and when I thought of this I put my arm round my sister's waist, and said, without reflection—

" Dearest Gertie, I hope you will never give your heart to anybody in the way that poor Guy has given his to Meta."

Her first impulse, after I had thus spoken, was evidently to be vexed, and to remove my arm from its position, but milder feelings soon succeeded, for she let the arm be, and only answered with a light laugh—

" Unless I could meet with a second Harold Wyke, I presume, Ethel? In such a case, you would consider it safe and even desirable for me to love, as you do, with all my powers of loving ?"

" My darling," I said, foolishly enough, "you must know there is only one Harold Wyke in the universe. I wish for your sake it were otherwise. Amongst all the men that remain, I shall never deem any one worthy of my dearest sister."

" Then your dearest sister had better become an old maid," she replied, still jesting without one atom of the spirit of mirth. " I am content that so it should be, Ethel ; but now we will speak a little of Guy. This history mamma has been telling him has evidently affected him deeply. What do you think he will do ?"

" Go down to see Meta, for one thing, and ask her to wait till he is in a position to marry her for another. One need not be a fortune-teller to predict so much as that, Gertie."

" And when she refuses him, as of course she will, what then, Ethel, the seer ?"

" But not the seer where the undisciplined

passions of a passionate man's heart are concerned, Gertie. He may fret himself into a consumption, or he may, though God forbid, become a reckless libertine. This I am sure of—Meta's final rejection of him will work some wondrous change in him—will never leave him as it found him."

" I think so, too.   But is it certain that she will reject him ?"

" She will either reject him at once, and for ever, which she ought to do, or, for the gratification of her own miserable vanity—I call it vanity, though Meta repudiates the word as applicable to herself—she will keep him hanging on till a more desirable husband comes forward. But hark, Gertie, I believe that is Guy's step on the path behind us."

It was.   He had succeeded in throwing off his selfish cares and anxieties for the time, and was anxious to atone to me for his apparent neglect and want of sympathy.

We remained in the garden together, all

three of us, chatting pleasantly, and occasionally quite cheerfully for nearly an hour. Guy had all his Cambridge life to tell us about—his companions—his hard reading—his hopes of gaining some creditable honours before his college career was ended, and the church interest promised him by one particular friend as soon as he should need it. And we, in our turn, had to tell him everything not contained in our letters, that had happened at Graybourne since he went away, especially how the vicar and myself had come to fall in love with each other, what black arts I had used to win a man whose shyness of women was only exceeded by his goodness, and finally in what terms I had made the offer, as he was very positive—this saucy brother of mine—that Mr. Wyke must have left that part of the courtship to me.

Gertie complained of the night air, and went in doors a few minutes before Guy and myself. The moment she had left us he grasped my arm with an eager, nervous clutch, that was far from agreeable as a mere physical sensation, and exclaimed in a voice that contrasted oddly with the pleasant, bantering one he had hitherto adopted:

" Ethel, how could you come away and leave her, perhaps dying, amongst total strangers, and with her little dead child still under the same roof with her? I think it was almost cruel."

" I am sorry, dear Guy," I said, trying to show no resentment at his glaring injustice, " that you should disapprove of anything I have done. In this case, I cannot stoop to defend myself, simply because the accusation does not reach me even obliquely. I think Gertie was right about the air being cold. Let us follow her in."

He did not say another word, and mamma ordered me peremptorily to bed as soon as we entered the dining room.

I know the rest sat up talking till long past

midnight, for I could not sleep, and I heard them all pass to their respective rooms a few minutes before one o'clock. The thought came to me then a little depressingly, in spite of my exceeding happiness, that already I was looked upon as apart from the home circle, and a member of another family than my own.

  ✰ ✰ ✰ ✰ ✰

We were married very quietly, as became both my present station and future position. Mr. Wyke had interfered in none of the arrangements connected with the wedding beyond a timid request, made to me privately, that if Mrs. Arnott must be amongst the guests at the breakfast, I would manage to have her seated as far from him as possible. And so we contrived that Walter Kenyon (who had paid the vicar and myself the compliment of remaining at Graybourne on purpose for the wedding, and was to start for Brighton the same day), should have the fair widow next to him, while on her other side, in case this first gentleman failed to pay her sufficient attention, we placed the clergyman who had performed the ceremony, and was to stay at the vicarage and do duty for his friend during our month's absence.

By these means we pretty well secured the sensitive bridegroom from any special attacks from his too lively enemy, for although it was easy to see that Walter responded grudgingly to every call upon his politeness and gallantry made by Mrs. Arnott, because one who made no such calls sat in her quiet, dignified loveliness on the other side of him, still he was too much of a gentleman, and man of the world, not to bestow the attentions which were exacted with such a confident assumption of his delight and pleasure in paying them; and whenever through forgetfulness, or because he had won Gertie to listen with a little more than her usual graciousness to his beguiling voice, Mr. Kenyon failed in rendering the amount of homage the imperious widow believed her due, she had only to turn to her other neighbour who, elderly bachelor as he was—much older, dear reader, than Mr. Wyke —seemed really captivated, for the time being, by the pretty face and sparkling gaiety of the lady of Primrose Cottage.

Jane Norton (who had been to her own intense enjoyment my second bridesmaid), we committed to the especial care of Guy, while the Miss Downings and Mrs. Luke were supposed to receive their share of general attention, the husband of the latter being in high spirits, and talking glibly during the greater part of the breakfast to any lady whom he found free to listen to him.

I suppose it all went off very well; I never heard of a wedding breakfast that did not; but I know I was right glad when it was over; the healths drank, the speeches made, my bridal finery taken off, and mamma, Gertie, and Guy seated for one short half-hour in a little half-smiling, half-tearful group, around me.

Then came the farewells, which were only the least bit agitating and painful after all, for I was coming back in a month, and my home would be close to the home I was leaving, and they knew—these dear ones who loved me—that no earthly destiny could wear a fairer, brighter promise than mine.

And so they let me go from them at last with smiles and blessings on their lips; and my husband, seeing I was a little white and trembling, lifted me tenderly into the carriage that was to take up Maggie and her nurse at the vicarage; and as we drove from the midst of the hand-waving group at the gates, he pressed me to his heart, and whispered in a voice of such earnest feeling that it thrilled through me:

"I am asking God, my dearest, to make me more worthy of the precious gift He has given me!"

CHAPTER VII.

UNFORTUNATE RESULT OF A LEGACY.

WE went to one of the fairest as well as one of the mildest spots in the Isle of Wight. We said when we first beheld its unrivalled loveliness, and inhaled its soft yet bracing air, that it was impossible but that our darling should grow well and strong here. She was so happy too, so joyous, so full of gay childlike spirits, that even nurse began to look less grave, and to talk, as she had of late quite ceased to do, of the time when Miss Maggie should be a grown up young lady.

As for the father, his full and perfect contentment, his deep satisfaction both in his little daughter's improving health, and in myself as his daily companion, seemed something beyond the reach of ordinary language to describe. How well I remember those first few days at Ventnor, our mornings spent upon the open, sparkling beach, where we could watch the crested waves come dancing in, and lazily count the white-sailed fishing vessels, and look up dreamingly at the intense, cloudless blue of the sky above us, and sometimes join with Maggie in an energetic search for shells and pebbles, and sometimes leave her to hunt for her ocean treasures alone, or with nurse, while we sat together and talked and talked, as foolish lovers do, and caressed our new found happiness as if it were a sentient thing, and wondered again and again how we had managed to exist before we knew and loved each other.

Then, in the afternoons, our delicious rides along the beautiful undercliff where nature appears to have congregated, in a most lavish mood, all its varied and countless forms of loveliness, or our extended excursions to Blackgang and Shanklin, and other famous spots, which struck me at that time, and I think would strike me always, as having a quite peculiar charm belonging to them, that lingers tenaciously about the heart when the eye has ceased to behold them.

And then, last of all, our dim, quiet, enchanting evenings, either wandering again in the dusky twilight through some silent and unfrequented woods, where the rustling of the myriad leaves around us, made a music I always loved, or sitting by our own open window listening to the softly plashing waves against the pebbly shore, recounting our enjoyments of the day, and pleasing ourselves with the thought of how soundly and sweetly our tired Maggie was sleeping after them.

During these first days of novelty and ever varying amusement, I was really too happy, too selfishly happy, I suppose, to suffer any anxieties connected with others beyond our immediate circle, to enter into my mind. My husband and his great love for me seemed as much just yet as my heart could hold, and I felt as if I had a right for this little while to enjoy the good that had been given me wholly, fully, and without a thought that would have cast a shadow over its perfect brightness.

I am far from saying that I was unblameable or even excusable in so feeling, but this I know, that there is in life a certain kind and degree of happiness (rare indeed as the four leaved shamrock, which is supposed to confer a blessing on those who find it), that while possessed must necessarily make us selfish even against our will, by filling the heart and soul entirely with its own radiant light.

And such a happiness, in kind and degree, was that which I experienced in the first blissful conviction of belonging for ever to him I so deeply loved and honoured, and in knowing, not believing only, but knowing, that I was the very sunshine and joy of his life.

But, in spite of my partial intoxication, I was not mad enough to expect to live for ever in this paradise of the heart. I knew that by and bye there would come a descent from the flowery mount, and that I, like the rest of earth's wandering children, must look out for some desert roads and some thorny paths, where no roses bloomed nor any voice of nightingale was heard.

I knew all this, I repeat, well enough, but I don't think I realized it very clearly, or dwelt upon it as applicable to myself, for above a minute at a time, until, in less than a week after our arrival at Ventnor, I received my first letter from home.

And here I must explain that I had left directions with Gertrude to send cards, and a long letter I had written on the eve of my marriage to our relative and benefactor, Mr. King, who had been for more than six months away from England—staying at one of the German spas for his health. My reason for not giving him earlier intelligence of my engagement was the fear of his imagining that I expected a wedding present from him, and as his liberality towards the whole family had already been so great, I should have disliked particularly exciting any notion of this kind. So I only wrote at the last moment, knowing that long before he received my letter I should be a wife, and the period for receiving marriage gifts would be over. And, truly speaking, I had thought no more of the eccentric old gentleman from the hour of writing that letter till the one in which I held my mother's open in my hands.

After a few affectionate expressions of satisfaction and pleasure in the state of beatitude my letters home had described, mamma thus wrote:

" You will be shocked, my dear Ethel, to hear of the almost sudden death of our kind friend and relation, Mr. King. He died at Baden-Baden the very day before your wedding, away from all his friends, poor man! and having apparently derived no benefit to his health from his exile amongst strangers. We were surprised yesterday by a visit from his executor and man of business, who, indeed, was the first to bring us the sad news; but we were still more surprised when this gentlemen informed us that our dear Guy is Mr. King's principal legatee. To you and Gertrude he has left a trifling annuity, sufficient to have made work unnecessary had you both remained single. To other friends and connections he has also bequeathed insignificant sums, but the fortune altogether that has thus unexpectedly come to your brother will amount, the lawyer tells us, to at least thirty-five thousand pounds. Now, my dear Ethel, I foresee plainly what your first thought and apprehension will be on reading this intelligence, and of course I can only acknowledge that they are justified by what has actually occurred. Our dear, impetuous Guy started for Devonshire a few hours after he became aware of his good fortune. That he will propose at once to Meta there is little doubt; but this, far from surprising me, is what I have always felt inevitable from the moment he first spoke to me of his wild and extraordinary love for her. Also, I have ever felt a positive conviction (except during those few hours when I believed she might have entangled herself in an engagement to Mr. Hallam) that sooner or later she must become Guy's wife;

and hence the indulgence and tenderness, and even affection I have invariably striven to maintain towards her, even when I am sure it has appeared to you and Gertie, you especially, that she little merited such consideration from any of us.

" I was quite unsuccessful in exacting any definite promise from your brother before he left home, but I did implore him not to be beguiled into sacrificing his chance of distinction and honours at Cambridge, and in abandoning the sacred profession to which he has hitherto looked forward. At their ages they can afford to wait a few years—indeed, it would be the height of imprudence for Guy to marry yet, and I have told him that Meta can have a home with us for as long as she herself pleases. Your sister will not hear of giving up her pupils before Christmas, nor would she then, she says, but that they have not answered her expectations. You shall hear again, my love, the moment I have any

news from Devonshire. We all unite," &c.,
&c., &c.

" There, read it, Harold," I said, passing
over the letter to my husband as soon as I
had taken in its full import—" read it, and
tell me if you don't agree with me that Guy's
' good fortune,' as mamma calls it, will turn
out to be the greatest misfortune that could
have happened to him?"

I regret to confess that all my pity for Mr.
King, all my gratitude for what he had done
for us, were wholly lost sight of, for the time,
in my overwhelming annoyance at the
thought of the madness I knew my brother
would be running into.

" Pray don't excite yourself, my darling,"
said Mr. Wyke, observing, I suppose, how
flushed I was, as he gave me back the letter.
" Guy will surely respect his mother's wishes,
and simply engage himself to his cousin for
the present. If she remains true to him for

three years, it will be some guarantee that her character has improved. Even you must acknowledge this, my little Ethel."

And because he kissed and soothed me, and told me I ought to be grateful for the increase of wealth to our family, and that he should insist on my share being given up to Gertie until she married, I suffered him to believe that I was comforted, and that I accepted, for the present, his view of the case.

My kindest, dearest, most beloved husband! how could any sorrow seem heavy to me while those tender arms were around me, that loving voice whispering its fond, caressing words in my ear!

So for a few more sunny days I glided gently down the stream of present happiness, only now and then, when I happened to be quite alone, recurring uneasily to the subject of mamma's letter, and picturing at such times the wooing and the winning in course of progress at Salem Cottage. Always when

Harold returned to me I had a joyous smile to welcome him, and he was satisfied that my anxious mind was at rest.

It was, I believe, about the sixth morning after my first news from home that a letter was delivered to me, as we sat at breakfast, addressed by Guy, and bearing the Devonshire post mark.

" Finish your breakfast before you open it," said my husband, who could not have been so confident of Guy's discretion after all —" you are quite agitated now, Ethel, and I shall scold if a bit of that chicken is left on your plate—now, my child, oblige me."

And he took the letter, which was a very thick one, gently from my hand, and kept it beside his own plate till I had choked down the last atom of food on mine. Then he kissed me for my obedience—grudgingly yielded though it was—and gave me back the letter I was hungering for.

On breaking the seal I found that there

was a note, in a separate envelope, inside. This was from Meta, but I threw it down very disrespectfully, I am afraid, and read Guy's first.

I cannot give the whole of it here. It was too much a of rhapsody to be at all creditable to the writer, or interesting to the general reader. Guy was mad, and he wrote like a madman who has not even the little reason left to know that others cannot sympathize with the freaks of his insanity. The pith of the letter, and all that at first my indignant eyes could clearly make out, was this—

"I am married to Meta. I am the happiest and most enviable being in the whole world. You, who are so blest yourself, Ethel, must wish me joy, and love with your whole heart the sweet, angel sister, I have given you."

Following this were numerous details and

explanations, all intended to justify the indecent haste with which the wretched marriage had been contracted; but of course without a word from Guy—the infatuated boy-lover of an unworthy woman—it would have been easy to understand that on his part the fear of opposition from his family, and perhaps of change hereafter in Meta's own sentiments, had been his guiding motives. On her part, I supposed his wealth had tempted her to become his wife, and so raise herself at once from the lowly and dependent position into which, through her son's death, she had again fallen.

My new sister's letter was very brief, and a singular contrast to her husband's. She announced coldly enough the fact of her marriage, by special licence, at Yardley church, to my brother, and added somewhat insolently, I thought: "I have only made one stipulation with Guy, who has really taken my breath away by his eagerness to convert me into Mrs. Beamish, and that is that he shall give up all thoughts of entering the church. He has now no need for it in a pecuniary point of view, and, as I always told you, I should make a wretched wife for a clergyman.

" As my health is still very delicate, we are on our way to Brighton for the honeymoon, Guy having obtained an advance from Mr. King's executor for all present necessities. After this, we may go to Lindenhurst for a little while, until the whole property is realized and invested, and we shall have determined on our future residence. As Guy cannot be a clergyman he wishes to become a country gentleman. With kind regards to your excellent husband,

"Believe me, dear Ethel,

"Your affectionate sister,

"META BEAMISH."

I gave my husband time to read both these

letters, looking over his shoulder as he did so. Then snatching them from him I tore them into a hundred fragments, exclaiming passionately:

"Guy is a fool! and I won't pity him or break my heart for him whatever he may suffer."

"Hush, child," said my kind monitor, gently, and laying his hand on my sinning lips, "you will not break your heart, I trust, because that is not your own, but my possession; but you will certainly pity Guy (as the strong should ever pity the weak), when repentance and sorrow come to him. He has given up a high and holy vocation for a human love, which, in his hour of need, will surely fail him. Ethel," my husband added, gravely; "instead of being angry with your misguided brother, you should set yourself earnestly to pray for him, for he has 'sown the wind,' and he must, sooner or later, 'reap the whirlwind.'"

"He is mad and a fool," I said again in my exceeding bitterness of spirit, which refused to be admonished or set right. "A boy of twenty, just beginning his college life, knowing no more of the world than a baby, sensitive and impressionable as a romantic girl of fifteen; only half educated—a pretty person truly to assume the responsibilities and duties of a husband, and a husband, above all, to a woman like Meta!"

"But, dear Ethel, the thing is done," urged my patient companion again, "and all the fretting and railing in the world could not undo it. Guy has chosen his own path, and if he has to tread it with bleeding feet and a breaking heart—we will suppose the worst—at least let us hope that it will be leading him in a right direction. Happiness with one he has taken to his heart instead of God and duty, would, in my estimation, be a much worse thing for him than the misery you seem to anticipate."

"Well, well," I said, fretfully, and most

ungratefully; "he is not your brother, and you do not understand that woman, who has become a bride before her little child is cold in his grave, as I do."

Then, my dear husband, wounded and tired out by my ill-temper, rose slowly, and left me to myself and my rebellious murmurings.

When I had wearied of these and the floods of hot tears which nearly blinded me, I rang the bell and enquired for nurse and Maggie. If they were still at home I would go down to the beach with them, trusting that my husband would join us there, as soon as he had forgiven me my unkindness and passion.

But I received for answer, that Mr. Wyke had taken out Maggie himself, leaving word that he should not be back till dinner time.

And this was a specimen of the first fruits, as far as I was personally concerned, of my brother Guy's luckless marriage.

CHAPTER VIII.

THE DEMON THAT CAME TO ME.

As I had the grace to acknowledge, as soon as I could speak to my husband alone, how wrong and foolish I had been, and to beg him to forgive me (which he did with a very tender caress, and the kind of soothing one bestows on a wayward child)—of course, it was soon all right again, outwardly at least, between him and me. And when I say "outwardly," I do not refer in the very smallest degree to my ever indulgent and noble minded husband, who, I am quite sure, forgot all but the pain I had suffered from the moment I had confessed my fault to him, and he had kissed away my tears. I refer solely to myself, and to the wrong twist which had somehow or other got into my mind on that day that I received the news of my brother Guy's marriage.

It was one of those things that we can never wholly account for, but which probably enters into the experience of at least half the feminine portion of the human race. A sudden shadow coming between us and the sunshine, and the sunshine, though really unaltered, though falling upon us as brightly and warmly as ever, yet never seeming to us quite the same again.

It was not that after the first rude shock and disgust which Guy's exceeding folly had inspired, I was continually thinking and lamenting over this folly. I did certainly

think a good deal of it, and my thoughts on
the subject were never pleasant ones ; but, as
I have tried to express above, the mischief it
had done me was of a more purely personal
nature, and referred to the darkening of that
unclouded happiness with my husband which
I had enjoyed before those ill-fated letters
came.

Let me repeat once more, that with all this
my dearest Harold had himself nothing to do.
In attention, in tenderness, in every kind of
affectionate consideration he was wholly unchanged—I could not but admit so much even
then—and yet, because my mind had got out
of tune, enervated, I suppose, at first by its too
exceeding contentment, and then startled and
shaken by the news which had so terribly
distressed me; because of this, I say, I began
stupidly and wickedly to distrust my husband,
by allowing suspicions to creep into my
jealous heart that he had, after all, only
chosen me as his wife because Maggie loved

me, and he believed I should make a good and affectionate mother to her.

I cannot remember either the day or the hour when the first miserable suggestion of this kind came to me in a concise and definite form.   I am sure it was immediately after the day I have last spoken of, when the father had taken out his little daughter and left me alone for the whole of the morning.   It is true he told me, on his return, that he believed I should recover sooner and better by myself, with my own judgment and conscience to guide me, than if he remained near me ; and quite true also that I accepted this explanation, and thought myself satisfied with it.   But on looking back at it all now, I imagine that this little apparent,—only apparent,—neglect, was really the beginning of my jealous and torturing fancies.

A few days of cold, bleak weather setting in suddenly, and while we were still wholly unprepared for them, not only threw Maggie back considerably, as regarded the strength she had gained, but brought on a distressing little cough, every sound of which, I soon perceived, was a dagger in the father's heart.

"Anything but a cough," he said to me one evening, when our child was in bed, and we had drawn our chairs to the fire that had now become really necessary, "her poor mother's illness commenced with just such a cough as Maggie seems to be getting. She must not move out, Ethel, while these cold winds last. You will manage to amuse her indoors for a day or two?"

"I will do my best," I replied, "but you must not allow yourself to be over-anxious now, having kept up hope so long. I don't see anything very alarming in Maggie's cough at present. All children are subject to colds and coughs in the autumn."

I spoke thus with the sincere intention of lessening his evident uneasiness. I loved my husband far too dearly not to wish to comfort

him in any anxiety he might have, even while
I thought I had deceived myself as to the
extent of his love for me.   But it may be that
I did not speak quite as warmly or sympa-
thetically as usual, for instead of receiving
consolation from my words he only sighed, as
if his heart was too full for any further discussion of its pain, and immediately after proposed reading to me.

"I shall never be either a comfort or a
help to him except inasmuch as I am of use
to Maggie," was the bitter thought that then
rushed into my mind; and although my
husband read aloud a most interesting book
till our supper was brought in, I am not aware
of having understood a single word of it.

For several days, acting upon the father's
wishes, I kept Maggie entirely to the house,
devoting myself, during this time, wholly to
her amusement, and not stirring from the
hot room where she was imprisoned until she
went to bed and I could be of no further use

to her. My husband did remonstrate several times against this, assuring me that I should injure my own health, and that Maggie could not want me for the whole day; but because he did not insist on taking me out, I was stubborn and self-willed about it, pretending that I did not like the cold winds any better than Maggie, and that I had seen all I wanted to see of Ventnor. Sometimes, when my little step-daughter was in bed, I would propose a stroll by the sea for half-an-hour, but as the father, on these occasions, was generally either absent and preoccupied, or full of anxious questions as to how much or how little Maggie had coughed during the day, the walks did me no good, and I often regretted having suggested them.

And yet I did not see much of my husband at this time. He had discovered an old college acquaintance leading a quiet bachelor life in a pretty cottage at Bonchurch, and nearly every morning from the period that

Maggie began to droop, he used to leave us immediately after breakfast, and either sit or walk with this gentleman till it was time to come home to dinner. Not unfrequently he would send word that we were not to wait for him, as he and his friend were going on a long excursion, and he should only be back to tea.

"Why does papa leave us so much?" said Maggie to me one day, "it isn't half so nice when he is away, because you look dull, mamma darling, and I think my not being well is vexing you by keeping you from papa. Ask him not to go out so often."

With my dear child's artless words ringing in my ears and finding too true an echo in my heavy heart, I remarked to nurse that evening on Mr. Wyke's constant absences, and added, in a jesting tone (that the old woman might not divine how seriously I took the matter):

"You see he has soon grown tired of my

society, nurse. I daresay the first Mrs. Wyke understood and suited him better."

" Bless your heart, t'aint that at all !" was the quick reply, accompanied by a look of surprise that was far from displeasing to me, " master goes out because he just can't bear to hear Miss Maggie's cough, and he knows she's safe and happy with you, ma'am   Once set that blessed child on her legs again, which we shall do, please God, when the wind shifts round to the west, and you'll soon see whether master won't care for your company. Why, ma'am, begging your pardon and you yourself having begun the subject, a person with only one eye could see that he fairly dotes upon you."

How I loved the old woman at that moment. How wise and good and discriminating I thought her. And, shall I confess my foolishness ? I actually made a pretence of wanting to breathe the fresh air to run into the town alone, though it was then dark, to buy the dear old soul a new cap ribbon. I met my husband as I came back returning from his friend's cottage ; and, still brimming over with the intense gladness nurse's observation had excited, I seized his arm eagerly, exclaiming,

" Oh, I am so pleased. I did not expect you home for another hour. Do, dear Harold, come to the beach with me; there is a moon, you see, and I have not been out before all day."

I acknowledge it frankly—I had for the moment entirely forgotten poor little Maggie. I was but a young wife, loving my husband with a passionate devotion, and for many, many weary days I had been questioning the reality of his attachment, except in a quiet fatherly sort of way, to myself. Now a new hope and trust had sprung up in my heart, and it was surely natural that at the moment I came face to face with him I should think of no one but our two selves in the whole universe.

Equally natural was it that his first thought should be for the sick child he had not seen since early morning, and whose ominous cough, ever striking like a knell on his frightened ear, had in fact (as nurse surmised) driven him from home. He had no doubts of my affection; no suspicion that I questioned his; if my manner ever appeared cold or strange to him, the most he believed was that I was too anxious about my brother's destiny to give all the thought and sympathy I should otherwise have done to Maggie's indisposition.

So, after a brief assertion that I ought not to have been out then so late alone, he said, and, I fancied, rebukingly :

" But about Maggie, Ethel; you have told me nothing yet. Is she any better ? has she coughed less ? does nurse think there is the least favourable change in her ? The wind got round to the west this afternoon, and I have been hoping ever since that she may have felt the benefit of it."

He could not see the tears that rushed to my eyes, he could not guess the chill that had struck to my foolish heart, which had so thirsted for one little word of love addressed to me—his wife—who had been a long day without him. He only heard, and no doubt wondered at, the cold, listless tone, in which I replied to his numerous and eager questions:

"I think Maggie is about the same. I have not heard nurse say that she has observed any change in her. I am sure she was much worse than she is now before we came here, and yet you never seemed anxious then. What has come over you?"

"She had no cough before, Ethel," he answered gravely; "but perhaps I am as ready to exaggerate her danger now as I have hitherto been to ignore it.   Let us hope that the milder weather will build her up again. You are shivering, my child, so I don't think I can indulge you in your walk by the sea, after all.   Better come home and have something warm, and then I can ask nurse more particulars about Maggie."

I was quite as ready now to go home as he was, and walking silently by his side I kept crushing nervously the little paper parcel in my pocket, thinking what a fool I had been, and wickedly wishing that I was in danger of death instead of Maggie.

CHAPTER IX.

THE PLEASURES OF A SORE THROAT.

NEITHER the predictions of nurse, nor the hopes of Maggie's father, were destined to disappointment, for with the return of the mild weather our little invalid's cough quite left her, and we were once more enabled to enjoy our walks and our drives as at the first. Now that my husband's anxieties about his darling were, for the time being, lulled to rest, his wife took her place again as his constant companion, his principal object of solicitude, and his unmistakably chief source of enjoyment and happiness.

What more could I have desired to render my contentment perfect? Was it possible that any haunting doubts or fears could still show their dark faces even on the threshold of the home which such love as ours was brightening?

If I say it was, I shall certainly be condemned as the most unreasonable, ungrateful, fanciful creature in existence, and perhaps told that so far from deserving a husband like my Harold, I ought to have been sent to school again, and made to sit under the shadow of Minerva until I had learnt at least as much of wisdom as should have enabled me to take care of my own peace of mind, and not squander it away as a thing that at any time could be renewed or mended up.

But alas! alas! how frightfully and madly the most of us in this world do trifle with our happiness, and suspect not what we are doing until the happiness is gone, and in its place we find a cup that must be drained to its dregs, filled with bitter wormwood and gall.

Of course I was not insensible to the pleasure of having my husband constantly with me again, of being petted, and caressed, and loved by him every hour of the day, of seeing with my own eyes that Maggie was now put quite in the back-ground, and that he was content to let her, at any time, wander apart from us with her nurse, that he and I might be alone together to renew our lovers' talk, or to build, in concert, shemes and plans for the future. Of course, I repeat, I enjoyed all this intensely—with a pleasure that, from its very excess, was often akin to pain—but I enjoyed it as a school-boy enjoys a bright summer holiday, ever pursued with a conviction that it must soon come to an end, and the black Monday dawn like a grim, unrelenting destiny, upon me again.

"You certainly cannot be well, my child," Harold said to me one evening as we sat side by side in the twilight; "your spirits have become so variable lately, and you often look —as I think you are looking now—as if you had some great weight on your mind. Is Guy's foolish marriage distressing you still?"

"Not much," I replied truthfully, for whatever I might feel on that subject, it was not to be compared to what I felt on the one affecting my individual happiness. "Not much, indeed, Harold, and you must not begin to take fancies about me as well as about Maggie. I am really in excellent health."

"Perhaps pining for home, then?" he continued, drawing me nearer to him, and fondly stroking my hair. "Is my darling tired of her holiday, and wanting to be at work again? new work it will be now, you know, Ethel, the work of a clergyman's wife, instead of a schoolmistress. Do you expect to like the change?"

"Very much," I said; "but I am in no hurry to begin. I am very happy here with you, Harold. While you love me, I could never pine for anything beyond."

"While I love you!" he repeated, in a strange tone, at least I thought it strange; "child, child——!" but here he broke off suddenly, letting drop the hands he had clasped almost passionately, as he first began to speak, and got up and paced to and fro in the room.

I was almost tempted then to exclaim, "oh, my husband, I am a fool, an idiot, a self-tormentor of the maddest kind. I see your love for me; I believe in it; I feel it; every minute of the day brings me some new proof of it; and yet I am wretched, because I have admitted into my heart a mean jealousy of the little daughter you have every right to cherish and hold dear."

The words were on my lips, and I had half risen to say them when my husband stopped abruptly in his walk, and came and sat down again beside me.

"Ethel," he asked, "what makes you think that I have only fancies about Maggie now, when it was you yourself who first pointed out to me the danger she was supposed to be in?"

No fear of my making any confessions after this. I wrapped my dreary pride about me, and answered, in an indifferent tone—

"I was told she was in a dangerous state, and my own observation led me to think badly of her at the time I first mentioned the sub-ject to you. Since we have been here her very remarkable improvement has inclined me, as well as nurse, to form a different opinion. Therefore it was that I spoke of your recent anxieties as fancies."

"God grant that you may be right in thus designating them," he said earnestly, adding immediately in a more cheerful voice: " and as long as she does not cough, I shall not suffer myself to become uneasy again."

A day or two after this, staying out too late in the damp air (for the autumn rains were now commencing), I caught a rather bad cold myself, and as it was accompanied by a sore throat I had no choice but to acknowledge my indisposition and submit to nurse's lectures and doctoring. At first, when I saw how anxious and fidgetty my husband was about this trifling ailment, I only laughed at him, and told him he was the greatest coward I had ever known; but as my sore throat increased, and his fears with it, so that at last he insisted on my taking to my bed and having a doctor, I began to experience a secret and wholly selfish pleasure in the extra care and petting of which I became the object, and to like my confinement to that dull room, and even my slight physical discomfort, above all things.

My husband was at any rate all my own now. He scarcely ever left my side, and when he did it was only to go out and bring me fresh fruit, or a new book, or something else that he thought might give me pleasure. He would sit and read to me by the hour together, never wearying as long as I seemed amused; or if my head ached, he would stand patiently over me bathing my temples, or just holding my hands, and only breaking the absolute silence which at such times he thought good for me, by an occasional term of fond endearment, rendered sweeter to my ever thirsty heart by the dear caress that came with it.

I was very, very happy, during those days of compulsory seclusion. I must have been a maniac indeed had I doubted of my husband's love then; had I not felt that, quite apart from Maggie and any idea that I might be a blessing to her, he clung to me and doated on me as his life's richest possession.

I remember well how I used to lie and watch some big elm trees that were always swaying their branches before my window, while I gathered together the many, many tokens, hourly recurring, of his precious affection, and hugged them to my grateful heart, and looked at them in every form and aspect they would take, and thought—often and often—that if I died now, before I could suspect or fear again, I should have had a full and abundant share of life's best happiness.

All this no doubt was very foolish for a wife, and a professedly sensible, matter-of-fact woman. Looking back upon it now through the vista of years—of years that have been thickly sown with the plain, practical cares, of ordinary human experience—I cannot but think that such ultra sensibility, such passionate craving for creature love, had in it a folly that partook of sin. And for all justification, or rather extenuation of my foolishness, I have nothing to plead but the weak woman's apology for greater and graver errors than mine—" I loved him so."

Before I was considered well enough to go out again, except in a covered carriage, the summer days that had followed us into autumn were really over, and we were all of us quite willing to begin thinking of home and its fireside enjoyments. Maggie had kept tolerably well during my illness, and the first day I went down stairs she acknowledged to me that she was getting tired of Ventnor and idleness, and wanted to return to Graybourne and commence her lessons once more.

" A good sign, papa," I said, turning smilingly to my husband as the child was nestling in my arms, " don't you think so ?"

" A capital sign for Maggie," he answered, cheerfully ; " but not for you, I think, Ethel. Our little girl imagines you are to teach her still, but I am nearly resolved on having a governess for her. I am sure you will not be equal to teaching at home, in addition to the parish duties you will now be expected to take some share in. I will not have my wife's strength overtaxed."

"No fear of that," I replied, confidently, "as long as I have you to fall back upon. Let me try at least to go on teaching Maggie myself. My darling would not like it otherwise, would she?"

"Oh! no, no, no," said Maggie, stoutly, "I don't think I could learn except with mamma—dear mamma, you won't give me up, will you?"

And this was the sweet loving child I had been jealous of.

I kissed her tenderly, and assured her that come what might I would be her only governess still. And the father laughed and kissed us both, and said that he saw plainly he was never again to be master in his own house. He should have chosen a wife who would not have cared a bit for her step-daughter, instead of one who joined with her in a league against the reigning authority.

The day before we went home I received a long letter from Gertrude, from which I give the following extract :—

"I was sorry that you wrote so warmly and indignantly to mamma on the subject of Guy's marriage ; it upset her very much for the time, and you might have reflected, dear Ethel, that the thing being beyond remedy, there could arise little advantage from commenting upon it severely, and especially from prophesying evil as its inevitable result. No one can feel more incensed at Guy's foolish act than I do ; but I keep my sentiments to myself, knowing that the expression of them could only give pain to mamma, while it would bring no modification of their bitterness to me. Mamma always expected, and was, therefore, prepared for this marriage, and had Guy chosen to take Betsy for his wife, I am quite sure his loving mother would have tried to think highly of that absurd young woman, and have given her at least a kind reception as a daughter-in-law. For you and me, who doubt and mistrust this German girl, let us wait and see how she will turn out. Prosperity, and a loving husband, may be more favourable to the development of her virtues than the opposite conditions have been. Lizzie Vivian tells me that she met her several times at Brighton, as Meta called on Mrs. Vivian, and that lady not only received her graciously, as Mrs. Guy Beamish, but invited her and Guy to an evening party, where the bride sang and looked lovely, and excited universal admiration. Mamma is very busy making preparations for their reception early next month. She never alludes now to Guy's having given up Cambridge and the church —indeed, I believe she is quite reconciled to the affair altogether, and you must try to remember, dear Ethel, that it is not the fashion at Lindenhurst to put on a long face when our new sister is alluded to, or to speak otherwise than affectionately and cheerfully at all times of Mrs. Guy Beamish. I believe there is a good deal of village gossip waiting for your ear, but this is not in my line, and I know Jane Norton would never forgive me if I anticipated her revelations in particular. Tell Mr. Wyke, with my best love, that we must talk when we meet about his most generous proposal in reference to Mr. King's legacy to you. I shall be very pleased to welcome you both home again. Mamma unites with me in fondest love.

"Ever your affectionate sister,

"GERTRUDE."

CHAPTER X.

HOME, SWEET HOME!

IT was a strange and indescribable pleasure, differing from all that had gone before it, that I felt on entering my new home and being saluted on all sides as its mistress.

And yet this pleasure referred infinitely less to any girlish triumph in my novel dignity, to any anticipations even of future peace and happiness to be enjoyed beneath my husband's roof, than to the very manifest delight which my husband himself experienced in leading me across his threshold, and in welcoming me to all that henceforth was mine as well as his.

We had mentioned to no one except our own servants the exact day of our arrival, so that we had that first evening entirely to ourselves; and it would be difficult to say which of the three appeared the most gladsome and light of heart.

Maggie and I ran about the garden for as long as we were permitted to stay out of doors, and then we joined the vicar in his cosy little study, where he had ordered a good fire to be kindled, and where we sat talking merrily for the rest of the evening and looking over the engravings of the Isle of Wight and other sea-side trophies which we had brought home with us. This being a very important occasion, Maggie was permitted to remain up to supper, and after that social and pleasant meal the servants were called in to prayers, and for the first time I had the gratification of seeing my dear husband act as chaplain in his own family, and of hearing him pray without the formula of the Church of England service.

I thought his extempore supplication very beautiful and simple—perhaps I should have thought the same had it been the most bungling and halting effort in the world, his lips uttering it—but I am sure, under any circumstances, I should have been deeply touched by the concluding words in which he thanked the Father he addressed—first for the new, precious gift, which had been bestowed on him to brighten his home, and secondly for the amended health of the beloved child to whom the angel of death had seemed to approach so near. Finally, he commended both wife and daughter solemnly, earnestly, and I think tearfully (for the firm voice seemed once about to break down), to the care and love and eternal guidance of the great God he desired his whole household humbly and reverently to serve, and then, with a blessing on the kneelers generally, the prayer was ended, the room cleared, and I was sobbing in my husband's outstretched arms.

"Harold—I am not good like you. I never felt my sinfulness and utter unworthiness as I am feeling them to-night, as you have made me feel them by your loving prayer for me. Oh my dear, dearest husband, teach me to be good and humble and righteous—teach me to be as you are."

And then there came a tender "Hush, darling! you must learn to lean on a firmer reed than I should prove; and amongst other things, my Ethel, I think we must both study well that solemn injunction—'little children, keep yourselves from idols!'"

      ✿   ✿   ✿   ✿   ✿

The Graybourne people, friendly and unconventional as in a general way they were, held still to certain customs and privileges in a most tenacious and exacting manner. For a bride to have come to dwell amongst them and not to have endured the two or three days' state receptions, the "at home" so respectable and time honoured that its origin cannot even be traced by antiquarians, would have been an offence and a wrong these simple country folks could never have forgiven. So, knowing I was in for it, I had long ago determined to have it over as soon as possible; and the third day after my return was fixed for the beginning of my penance.

I should naturally have liked to have had my sister with me just for the first day, but when I mentioned it to Gertie she looked so very much as if some one had offered her an emetic that I gave up my design at once, and wrote a little note on reaching home after my visit to Lindenhurst, to ask Jane Norton to come to tea that evening as I had a favour to beg of her. Perhaps I was just a little curious on the subject of the " particular intelligence" which my sister had hinted that Jane had to communicate, and about which I could get nothing more out of Gertie, when I saw her, than—" Jane will tell you herself. I would not spoil her pleasure in the narration for the world."

So Jane, who was invited for six o'clock, came to me, all flushed and radiant, at exactly four, and apologized for her bad manners by declaring it would take two hours at least to tell me everything she had been keeping for my private ear, not to speak of other gossip, which anybody who cared for it might listen to.

Seated snugly in my bedroom, and with the door fast closed upon us, I cut short the rhapsodies in which Jane seemed inclined to indulge herself first, on the subject of my return, by entreating her to begin her story, and have the private portion of it over before Mr. Wyke came in.

Then, as I saw some tell-tale blushes rising to my young friend's cheek, I took compassion on her and said—

"Jane, let me try and guess your secret. Mr. Burns has asked you to be his wife?"

She almost sprang off her chair in the amazement this clever guess of mine excited. Her crimson face was then hidden on my shoulder, as she whispered—

" But however, ever, ever, could you have imagined such a thing? and Miss Beamish promised faithfully she would not tell you."

"No one told me, dear," I replied, making her look up and meet my eyes—" I saw that this would be the end long ago. Do you like him truely and entirely, Jane? "

"Oh, how can I help liking him," she exclaimed with the most amusing naïveté— " when he has shown that he is fond enough of me to wish to marry me. Only think ! a little ignorant, stupid girl, without a penny in the world, and he so clever and so well off, and more than double my age."

Suppressing my inclination to laugh, I acknowledged that all this proved the gentleman to be quite worthy of her sincere affection, which I could no longer doubt that Jane had given in exchange for the obligations she enumerated—and then I enquired, half hesitatingly, for it really was a delicate matter to broach to Jane now, how her aunts—I took care to speak in the plural—liked the thought of her accepting Mr. Burns for a husband.

In a moment the blushes, and the gladness, and the sparkling animation, deserted the young face, and an expression of pain fell like a shadow over it, as she replied in a low, cautious voice,

"Oh, I can never forgive myself for having talked, even to you, as I did of poor aunt Harriet. If I had only known, or guessed! but how could I ? I must just tell you this now, and then I shall try to forget that I ever had a thought that could wrong my dear, good auntie. Mr. Burns spoke to them first, before he said a word to me. Aunt Harriet called me into her room one morning after he had been paying an immensely long visit down stairs, and asked me rather abruptly if I felt myself old enough and wise enough to have a house and home of my own. I said, 'oh dear, no, auntie, I should know no more how to manage servants, or carve joints of meat, or make up weekly accounts, than Blabberty Cuetsums.' Then, very gravely, though kindly, she replied, 'I am sorry to hear you speak so, my dear, because our friend, Mr. Burns, has paid you the great compliment of asking you (through us as your guardians) to be his wife, and if you can like him well enough, and overlook the fact of his age, both your aunt Dora and myself shall be very pleased and happy to see you so well provided for.' I leave you to judge, dear Mrs. Wyke, of the

effect this announcement had upon me. I am
quite sure it was at least twelve hours before
I saw anything straight again, but I managed
somehow to tell auntie that I would think
the matter over—she looked so white and still
that I thought she must want me away from
her—and then I went to my own room, and
had a good cry, and wished Mr. Burns, just
for a little while, you know, at the bottom of
the sea, and could not for the life of me think
what I ought to do to make aunt Harriet
happy, and get her into my place as regarded
Mr. Burns' kind intentions. By and bye,
aunt Dora came into my room, and I believe
somehow, though I did not utter a word to
guide her, she understood my perplexity.
In any case she told me in a very emphatic
manner, that she knew it was now aunt
Harriet's wish that I should accept Mr. Burns'
proposal, and added that he was coming to
tea in the evening, and would expect my
answer. Well, he came, and they left me

alone with him; and he was so kind, and gentle, and affectionate, and nice altogether, that I felt it would be very easy to grow fond of him; and so it was all settled, and I should be as happy as the day is long if I did not feel continually as if I had robbed aunt Harriet. She is excessively good and kind to me, and does all she can to appear as cheerful and contented as usual. Dear Mrs. Wyke, I have not said, mind, that she is otherwise; I would not say it, even to you, for the world, but every lot, I suppose, however bright, has some little speck upon it, and this is the speck on mine."

"It will not be there long, Jane," I said soothingly; "your aunt's dignity and strength of will must bring her triumphantly through a disappointment of this kind. And now, dear, we will dismiss that part of the subject for ever. Tell me when you are to be married."

"Oh, not till the spring," she answered

with a renewed fit of blushing. " Mr. Burns
wants to get his house, which is not a very
pretty one, refurnished from top to bottom;
and my aunts say they are in no hurry to
part with me, and indeed think me over
young to be married at all, only Mr. Burns is
such a favourite, and he tells them that his
surplus years ought to be reckoned on to mine
to make up my deficiency. Oh, and would
you like me to give Blabberty Cuetsums to
Maggie? dear, precious, soft lamb! I shall
be so sorry to see it go, but my aunts declare
that an engaged young lady, with all her
own under clothes to make, ought not to want
dormice to play with. Shall Maggie have
it ?"

" Maggie will be charmed with it no doubt,
Jane—but I hear my husband's voice in the
hall enquiring for me, so come down and see
him, and then you can tell us the rest of your
news at tea time."

The rest of Jane's news consisted of village

gossip, most of which would be uninteresting to the reader, with the exception perhaps of a current report to the effect that Mrs. Arnott had made a dead set at the elderly clergyman who had supplied Mr. Wyke's place, and in spite of her professed contempt for any but young and attractive men, had acknowledged openly that if this gentleman would ask her, she would not mind marrying him.

"And does anybody in Graybourne entertain an idea that he *will* ask her?" said my husband, with symptoms of his old shivering fits beginning to manifest themselves.

"Oh, yes," laughed Jane—"I have heard several declare that he was unquestionably smitten—and last Sunday he walked nearly all the way home with her, after church. Mrs. Arnott never missed either morning or evening service while he was here."

In the presence of our young guest Harold said nothing more, but when he was alone with me and the subject had nearly passed from my mind, he exclaimed with sudden energy : " If Mr. Leslie commits the egregious folly of marrying that hare-brained widow, I would be the first to vote him into a lunatic asylum."

Jane Norton consented gladly to be my companion during the two weary days that I had to sit in state and dispense cake and wine—it was the fashion then—to my numerous visitors.

The first day came the little doctor and his wife, the Miss Downings, some members of two or three other unimportant families who lived either in the village or near it, Mr. Burns, and the widow from Primrose Cottage. This last mentioned lady was gayer in her dress and livelier in her manners than ever. She talked a great deal about " that dear, delightful Mr. Leslie," who had proved such an acquisition to Graybourne, and whose loss, but that it was compensated for by Mr. Wyke's return, everybody would so deeply have deplored. One blessing, however, was that he had promised to come back ere long, and she for her part believed that it would be sooner than most people expected. I inquired casually of Jane Norton, in one of Mrs. Arnott's necessary pauses for breath, how old Mr. Leslie was supposed to be. "About sixty, I should think," was the reply; and then I could not resist turning with a smile to the fair widow, and asking her if, under any circumstances, she could ever make up her mind to the contemptible and ridiculous position of an "old man's darling." "Ah, I see you have a good memory, and are malicious, Mrs. Wyke," she answered lightly, but colouring a good deal. "If I were married to a clergyman, I would try to set the people around me a better example. Your husband is spoiling you as fast as he can. Tell him so, with my compliments, and beg him whenever he writes, to present my

most affectionate regards to his friend,
Mr. Leslie."

The second day I had Mrs. Hallam and
Alicia, lately returned from Clinton Hall,
and both looking worn and anxious, as
Edmund had not yet been heard of. After
them came the Vivians, who had only just
arrived from Brighton, and were full of Mrs.
Guy Beamish, and the impression she was
making in society. It was in a half jesting,
half serious manner, that Mrs. Vivian added,
in a whisper, aside to me, " and I quite place
it to the account of your fascinating sister-in-
law that our young friend, Mr. Kenyon, de-
clined accompanying us again to Fell House.
She has got him securely in her chains at
last, and I don't much think your brother
admires his very open devotion."

These words, carelessly as they were
spoken, haunted and distressed me during
all the remainder of that day, while visitors
kept coming and going, and (many of them

being strangers) I had to exert myself to play the agreeable hostess. In the evening I told my husband all that Mrs. Vivian had said, and though he replied, with a kind wish to quiet my fears, "don't listen to gossip, much less to scandal, from any one, Ethel," I believe he attached some importance to it himself, for he became very grave and thoughtful from that time; and once, awaking suddenly from a long fit of musing, he said:—

"If Walter Kenyon turns out ill, after all, I can never trust to the fairest promises or the most specious appearances again."

CHAPTER XI.

WATCHING AND WAITING.

DEEPLY interested as I was in the question of my brother's domestic happiness, and watchful as this interest naturally made me, I was enabled to discover very little either to allay or confirm my apprehensions during the few weeks that Guy and his wife remained at Lindenhurst. One thing was that my own occupations prevented me from going much amongst my relations at that time. The schools the vicar had succeeded in establishing required constant supervision, and at present I had no one but Miss Dora to cooperate actively with me in the work. It is true that she was a most willing and zealous helper, for from the date of her receiving religious impressions (which had been the simple secret of Mr. Wyke's frequent visits to her) she had given her whole heart as well as her whole time to labours in the good cause; but then her health was still delicate, and besides this, my husband always fancied everything better done when I had done the chief part of it. To please him I would gladly have worked, had my strength permitted, a thousand times harder than any woman had ever worked before, abundantly rewarded if he only smiled upon me, and said:

"My darling, I am content with you."

And then, too, I had Maggie to teach, and my house to order, and constant visitors to receive, so that altogether it was the rarest thing for me to have a couple of hours to spare, during any portion of the day, to run down to Lindenhurst.

Guy, indeed, came to see me tolerably often while he stayed in the neighbourhood; but if he talked, on these occasions, of his wife, it was only to praise her beauty or her grace, or her fascinations generally, and not a hint could I ever get from him as to whether he was really happy with her or the reverse.

Gertrude, who of course saw them frequently together, assured me that Meta behaved very kindly and affectionately to her husband, and added, for my consolation, that she believed everything was going on comfortably between them as yet.

As yet! Well, they had only been husband and wife for about six weeks, and it would have been hard and cruel indeed, if Meta could not have allowed the poor foolish boy, who had laid both his heart and his life at her feet, to have preserved his illusion for that little space of time.

Once I spoke, as if casually, to my brother of Walter Kenyon, asking him if he had not made that gentleman's acquaintance at Brighton. I am sure I was not mistaken in thinking that his face flushed and his lip trembled slightly as he answered with seeming carelessness—

"Oh, yes! a clever, attractive fellow, stopping with the Vivians—Meta's friends. She thought him agreeable, I believe, for she invited him to come to us at Christmas. We are to have quite a party, you know, as soon as we are settled in our new home."

This new home was a small estate which Guy had purchased in the county adjoining ours, and to which he and his wife removed after spending about three weeks at Lindenhurst.

And dating from their departure everything went on quietly and uneventfully both at the vicarage and at my former home until mid-winter. Then Gertrude's pupils left her, and as she had been for some little time out of health, she came to stay a week or two with me, prior to a longer visit which she had consented, reluctantly I am sure, to make at Abbeylands, the residence of Guy and Meta.

I gave Maggie a holiday and diminished even my out of door labours that I might devote myself as much as possible to my dear sister. Indifferently as her school had succeeded, miserably as, according to her own idea, all her plans of usefulness in life had failed, she still could not endure the thought of being left without some definite and prescribed work upon her hands. Long and stubbornly she had resisted my husband's generous desire to add my legacy from Mr. King to hers, but yielding at last, because Mr. Wyke would not be refused, she had positively no excuse for continuing to receive pupils or for calling herself a schoolmistress.

My mother too had been most anxious for her to give up working in that fashion; and altogether the tide had borne her away, but left her stranded on a shore which to her view was hopelessly barren and desolate.

"What can I do henceforth?" she used to say to me, as we sat sewing and chatting together by the bright fire of my pleasant parlour. "I have no duties like yours to occupy me, no husband to please, no child to look after, no house to direct. I am literally condemned to a life of shameful idleness."

"I am sure I shall be most grateful for your help in my parish work," I would reply to her, "and you can employ your leisure in any studies you please, sweetening them by the poetry you have learned to love, and which poor I have not a single moment for."

I remember well the occasion on which I said this (not altogether thoughtlessly either), and the shadow of something beyond mere pain that flitted over my sister's face as I spoke. I remember too her answering me after the lapse of several minutes, slowly and bitterly :

"If I studied ever so diligently it would be only selfish work in the end, and as for poetry, Ethel, my brief acquaintance with its allurements has sufficed for me. Whether I love it, or whether I love it not, I have put it aside for ever."

"Then come and work with me when you return from Abbeylands," I said entreatingly, " you know, dear, how I want help, and how thankful both Harold and myself will be to you."

"I will help you certainly, Ethel," she replied listlessly, " but I have neither genius nor inclination for teaching bible texts and setting round-hand copies. My own work in life has failed, and I shall never really take earnestly to any other."

So I said no more then, but waited to see

what healthful duties time would bring her—
my poor, proud Gertie! who quarrelled so
bitterly and relentlessly with her own heart
because she had discovered it to be human.

It was during my sister's stay at the vicarage
that Maggie first began to show symptons of
drooping again. I don't think I neglected
her, but she was necessarily less entirely my
companion than when we had no one visiting
us. Nurse too was busy with some work
which, against my desire, she insisted on
undertaking for me, and thus it came to
pass that Maggie remained out in the garden
one day when a drizzling rain was falling,
got wet feet, and began to cough and look
ill again.

Remembering all that I had suffered during
her illness at Ventnor, I certainly did tremble
with some purely selfish apprehensions the
very first time that little hacking cough smote
upon my ear. I was sitting with my husband
in his study at the time, Maggie crouched on

the hearthrug between us, and I earnestly hoped he had not caught the dreaded sound. He did not lift his head from his writing nor make any remark then, but in the evening, when the child was in bed and Gertie out of the room, he observed suddenly—

"Ethel, Maggie's cough has come back. Do you know how it has happened?"

My heart sank as I told him I feared she had got wet feet the day before, and that we had only discovered it when the mischief was done. He did not utter a word of reproach —I wished he would—but he looked miserably anxious, and continued restless and unable to settle to anything for the remainder of the evening.

Two days after this Gertrude started for Abbeylands, and another two days found Maggie laid on a sick bed, her disease violent inflammation of the lungs, and, even by the hopeful Mr. Luke, her life despaired of.

The urgent necessity for active exertion,

for never-ceasing watchfulness, alone kept me up at all, I am quite positive, at this time. Blaming myself in some measure for the terrible calamity that had befallen us, feeling convinced that in his heart of hearts my husband must be blaming me too, I could not be a daily witness to his unspoken despair and anguish, without maddening over the sight, and was yet afraid, with that vision of his anger against me between us, to venture upon the most feeble effort to comfort him.

Strange and unnatural as it may appear— loving each other as we did—we scarcely ever exchanged a dozen words during the whole day while that terrible agony of watching and waiting lasted. When my husband spoke at all he spoke kindly and tenderly as ever, and it was generally to entreat me to take rest, to leave the sick room, to think more of my own health than I was doing. But besides that my dear Maggie, when she was conscious, could not bear me away from her, I was resolved to atone for what I had helped to do by sacrificing even my life, if it were necessary, in striving to repair my fault and give her back to her father. My only consolation was to think that if she died I should die too, and that at the last he would pardon me and bless me. I never loved or worshipped him so utterly and blindly as I did at this time, when I felt he was putting me from his heart, and only tolerating my presence because I was still his wife, and to be kind and tender towards me was his duty.

So it went on, day after day, night after night, fever increasing, weakness increasing, pain increasing—life ebbing slowly but surely away. And now the father, unable I suppose to command his feelings, rarely came for more than a minute into the room where nurse and I watched beside the suffering, dying child— came and looked at her steadily for that little minute, looked at me with a strange, mournful, wistful glance, and then went out again.

" He is a'most beside himself," nurse used to say, "and will go clean mad, it's my belief, if neither God nor his wife can comfort him."

His wife would have died to have had the power to do it—willingly, joyfully—but she dared not lift a finger in the attempt with that shadow where it was.

And yet those words of nurse's haunted me distressingly, and I began to think that I ought, at any risk of having my own heart wounded, to do something, as a wife who was loved and trusted would naturally have done, towards soothing and consoling my afflicted and patient husband.

That night Maggie was quite conscious, and her breathing a trifle less laboured than usual. Mr. Luke had promised to come in, for the second time since morning, about nine o'clock. He considered her to be sinking fast, but he wished to try a new remedy that he thought might possibly mitigate the fever and render her last few hours easier if not painless.

I desired nurse to let Mr. Wyke know that the dear child was awake, and capable of speaking a few words at a time without much difficulty. This was about eight o'clock, and half-an-hour after receiving my message, when quite worn out myself, I had nearly dropped asleep in my easy chair by the bed, he came in, and immediately told nurse she might go down to her tea.

I had already placed a chair for my husband quite close to Maggie's pillow, so now I only drew my own a little back, and remained with my eyes closed that the father and daughter might speak together uninterruptedly.

At first he only leant over her and held the small, wasted hands, in his, stroking them very gently and fondly, and murmuring now and then such loving words as " Maggie, my darling !" or " my patient little girl." But by and bye, as he found her calm and disposed to listen, he began to talk to her of death and eternity, of Heaven and the white robes waiting there for the souls that had been washed and made clean in the blood of the Lamb, and when a little stifled sob or two mingled with his solemn words he took the child in his arms—the child so passionately loved—and asked her on what she built her hopes of joining that white-robed multitude.

Ah, I had no fear about my Maggie's answer. She and I had talked this great matter over many and many a time since she had called me mother, and I knew, beyond all doubt, that whenever the Angel of death might summon her, our loss would be her unspeakable gain.

Yet I listened with the deepest interest to her present catechising, and was affected above measure by the simple manner of her reply.

"1 am not afraid to die, papa," she

whispered, in her low faint accents, " because I expect that God will take me to Heaven and not let me suffer any more pain. And why I expect this is that He has promised to do it, and that I must believe what God has said."

" But, my Maggie," urged the father, " God has only promised this to the holy, the righteous, the very saintlike and good. Does my little girl feel that she has been always very good ?"

" No, no," came the louder and more stedfast answer, " but Jesus was good, good, and he puts his goodness round his children who love and try to serve Him, and so we get to Heaven. Dear papa, you taught me this long ago."

" But God himself has taught it you now, my darling," exclaimed the father in a voice that was both prayer and praise.

And then I knew that he needed not my poor attempts at comforting him. And feeling that to neither of them could I be of any further use, I wept silently in my hidden place, for all the time he remained beside Maggie in the room.

*   *   *   *

"What is it, nurse?" I cried, starting from a sleep that had seemed of half a century's duration, but had lasted in reality only four or five hours.

"It's morning, ma'am," she replied in such brisk and cheery accents that I was awake and sitting up in a moment, "and I couldn't help coming to tell you that our blessed child is better, and Mr. Luke says may do well yet. The new stuff he gave her last night, after you fell asleep and was carried by master's orders off to bed, had such a wonderful effect upon her that she got a beautiful night, the chest being relieved and the fever stopped; and she is quite another creature this morning."

" Thank God."   This was my first thought, but it was too intensely felt to be expressed audibly.   Aloud I said:

" And Mr. Wyke, nurse ? does he know it? is he with her ?"

" Bless you, he has been with her all night," she said, beginning to sob now, I suppose for joy, " and when the doctor came an hour ago and was so surprised and said Miss Maggie might get over it after all, and be a strong woman, I really thought poor master's feelings would have been too much for him.   But he knew Who to go to in his gladness, as he had known Who to go to in his sorrow. My dear, blessed master! such prayers as his are pretty sure to be heard."

For a moment I laid down on my pillow again and sobbed as if my heart were breaking. Nurse put my tears to the same account as her own, and so it did not matter, but my very soul was yearning over my husband and crying out against that cruel barrier, of whatever nature it might be, which at such a moment was keeping him from me.

I felt very faint and exhausted, but I got up, bathed my face, and went to Maggie's room. The father was in my seat by her bedside. He signed to me to move noiselessly as she was asleep, but as soon as I came near enough he took my hand very kindly and tenderly, and made me sit down close to him. I don't know what else he could have done, but I know that my sore and jealous heart was not satisfied, and because of this I uttered no word of sympathy or gladness, I sat in a half-sullen, half-pensive silence, watching Maggie's quiet slumbers, hating myself for not throwing my arms round my husband and showing him that, whatever shadow stood between us, his joy was *my* joy, and yet as incapable of doing it, or of manifesting anything but that cold, ungracious demeanour, as if my heart had suddenly changed to ice, and I was grieving instead of rejoicing over Maggie's amendment.

It did not make the matter better when I perceived that my husband was quite un-observant of this savage mood of mine; that, wholly wrapped up in his own deep thankful-ness and gladness, he took my sympathy and pleasure for granted, and laid to the account of my long watching and nursing the pale cheeks, and swollen eyes, and brooding aspect, which had in truth a less natural and legitimate origin.

As soon as nurse came up from her break-fast, he put his arm round me and drew me gently from the sick room, into my own, which I had recently left, and there, closing the door upon us, he asked me to kneel and join with him in thanking the Giver of all good for the unhoped-for blessing which had been at the eleventh hour granted to our prayers.

This was right, this was fitting, this was

what any pious father, under similar circumstances, would have done, and had my heart
been in a calmer state I should have been
glad to have been associated with my husband
in so holy and unquestionable a duty. As it
was, of the two who knelt, there was only one
who prayed, and when I rose up, the tears
were again streaming in torrents down my
face.

"My dearest," he said then, "I have been
mad and cruel to let you exert yourself as
you have done. It has been too much for
your strength, Ethel. Now I shall take you
in my own hands and have you properly
attended to. Remember, my child,—I, at least,
shall not forget it,—that our darling's restora-
tion is, under God, attributable to your
devoted care."

Then my husband laid me tenderly on the
bed, insisted on my not moving from it without orders, fetched me some breakfast which
I was compelled to eat, and finally told me

that Mr. Luke should see me when he came, and that he would himself, after that, go for my mother or Miss Dora to attend to the household duties which I should have to leave unfulfilled.

Well, I really felt physically ill enough to submit to all this without a dissenting word. I wanted to be alone and in darkness. I longed for sleep and oblivion of my self-created woes. My husband's very kindness distracted me, for was it not bestowed upon the patient slave who had helped to keep off the grim tyrant from his darling, his heart's delight, his precious Maggie? Oh, no doubt I should henceforth be esteemed as very precious also, since I had faithfully performed the work I had been converted into Mrs. Wyke to do. He could not choose but treat kindly, and cherish even affectionately, one whom he supposed had done her best to win back, at her own life's risk, the golden sunshine that had seemed to be fading for ever from his path. If I had committed an error I had now atoned for it, and he had accepted my atonement. Surely the esteem and frendliness and good feeling between us would henceforth be of a most calm and comfortable nature, and when this fever of the heart had worn itself out, no doubt I should become a very sensible and a very moderately happy wife and step-mother.

Do you think I was mad, now that I have thus exposed all the secret and bitter feelings that like an angry sea beat against my poor, restless heart on that memorable morning, as I lay weary and languid on my bed, after my husband had left me?

I think so, myself, for jealousy, when it drives its sharp and poisoned teeth into our weak human flesh, makes us madder for the time than the unfortunates who, with their reason wholly overthrown, can yet feel that the north wind is chill, and God's sun in the Heavens warm and bright, while we, who are jealous, see and feel nothing, either in earth or Heaven, beyond the fiery serpent whose coils are around us, and whose gleaming eyes are looking something worse than death into ours.

CHAPTER XII.

SORE HEARTS AT ABBEYLANDS.

I was ill enough to become Mr. Luke's second patient at the vicarage, and to keep my room and my bed for several days. The doctor said my strength had been overtaxed, and that absolute rest, and freedom from any kind of excitement, were, above all things, necessary for me. My mother and Miss Dora took it in turns to come and sit with Maggie (who was rapidly recovering), and to attend to my domestic duties. My husband divided his leisure time pretty equally, I think, between his little girl and myself; but he was obliged to be a good deal from home in consequence of my failing him just now, and some days I only saw him for a few minutes in the morning, and perhaps for about half an hour in the evening.

I could not complain of this. I knew it was inevitable; and whenever he was with me I had every reason to be satisfied with his tenderness and attention. Mr. Luke had assured him from the first that my indisposition would be a merely temporary affair, and so, of course, it would have been absurd of my husband to make the fuss he had made with Maggie, or even to be fidgetty and anxious as he had been when I had that sore throat at Ventnor.

We were getting to be old married people too, now, and it was high time we ceased to indulge in the sentimental follies excusable in young lovers.

Admire the wisdom that had come to me upon my sick bed. I could scarcely have got up a more creditable display had I returned to school and sat, in my ancient fashion, for the same length of time, under the shadow of Minerva. No one will doubt that I had become a zealous pupil of that beneficent goddess when I go on to relate what I did on recovering from my brief illness.

First of all, I ascertained from Miss Dora that she could continue her attendance on Maggie, who still required a good deal of care, if my mother would take up her abode at the vicarage, and thus afford me a holiday. I assured them both I wanted a little change and should like of all things to accept my brother's oft repeated invitation to Abbey-lands, now especially while Gertie was there. This settled, and the minor details of my journey arranged, I walked one morning into the vicar's study in my travelling dress and with my little carpet bag in my hand. The wisdom of this part of my proceedings consisted in my intention of surprising him into a display of his real feelings. If my going away would be a relief to him I could not fail to find it out; if it pained him to lose me for a week—I never contemplated being away longer—the discovery would be equally easy to me, and I should set forth with a lightened heart.

My husband was writing when I went in—it was his busiest hour of the day, but I had no choice, having to reach Boltby by twelve o'clock; he looked up as the handle of the door turned, opened his eyes very wide when he saw me, and said, with more curiosity, I thought, than anxiety in his voice:

" Why, Ethel, what is this? where are you going with that closely packed bag, and on such a cold morning?"

I had not been out of the house yet since my illness.

" I am going on a visit to my brother," I

answered as firmly as I could manage to speak; "I knew you could spare me, Harold, if mamma came, which she will do, to take my place. I feel the want of change very much. You do not mind, do you?"

I am sure, now, that it was pure and simple astonishment at the whole nature of my proceeding which hindered my husband from immediately answering me, which kept his gaze rivetted, as if by fascination, on my changing countenance, and at the same time brought so new a look into his own. But I thought then it was anger at my apparent contempt of his authority as a husband, and being suddenly struck with some conviction of the impropriety of what I had done, I hastened to add:

"I felt so sure of your being able and willing to spare me for a week, that I thought it just as well to make all my arrangements before consulting you. I rather fancied you might, if I gave you time to consider it, raise objections to my leaving home so soon after being ill, but that when you knew the matter was settled, you would agree with me as to the expediency of my getting this little change. I am sorry that I did not speak to you before, however, since I fear it has displeased you. Miss Dora will come every day as usual to see Maggie, and both her sister and herself will attend at the schools."

Here I paused and sat down for a moment, feeling really faint and a little out of breath.

"I am not displeased, Ethel," my husband said almost as soon as my explanation was ended; "only very much surprised. I quite believe, however, that you require change, and I am glad you have thought of something which will give you and your family pleasure. When do you start, and how?"

"The coach stops at Boltby at twelve o'clock. I shall only be two hours on the road. There will be a fly for me here in a quarter of an hour."

"And did you propose going to Boltby alone?"

"Why, yes, because I knew this was one of your busiest days —— "

My voice was getting rather unsteady now, and I stopped abruptly.

"Not too busy to keep me from attending on my wife," he said gravely, though very kindly, and seeming to study my troubled face as he spoke.

So we went as far as Boltby together, talking very little, and that only on general subjects, on the road.

My husband kissed me with all his wonted tenderness at the last; once I thought he was going to ask me to give up this journey; and as he put me in the coach and whispered, "God bless my dearest wife!" I fancied I saw something like a tear in his eye, which was quickly turned away from me. At that moment my heart smote me for what I was doing; I would have given worlds to have been able to undo it all ; to have sprung from that hateful coach, and implored my husband to take me home again, to have clasped the dear neck and told him how I loved him, how I worshipped him, even though the confession should have brought me no payment in kind. It was agony now to be leaving him, and leaving him of my own free will. I could not bear it ; I would not. Why should I ?

He was standing a little aside from the coach door, making room for packages to be stowed in. I got up ; I thrust my head from the window. The words which should release me and make me happy were on my lips, when suddenly Harold moved nearer to me, took my hand, which had been half stretched out to open the coach door, and said, with a faint smile—

" Maggie will miss her mamma cruelly just as she is getting about again ; but I may tell her that you will soon come back to her, may I not, dear ?"

I don't remember that I answered him at all, for the horn blew at that instant, the driver, red-faced and plethoric, scrambled up to his seat, the outside passengers followed, and away we all flew over the noisy stones, as fast as four swift horses could carry us.

If I cried, or if I laughed, if I sorrowed, or if I rejoiced during that two hours' lonely journey, matters not greatly now.   Be sure of this—I drank the cup that my own hand had mixed, and I drained it to the last mouthful.

*   *   *   *   *

If it were always true that the contemplation of other people's misfortunes lightened our individual griefs, then I am quite sure I should not have known that I carried a burden at all by the time I had been two days at Abbeylands.   And yet it was a fair, fair spot, and possessed of every external accessory to enjoyment; and there was plenty of laughter ringing through the lofty rooms, and music nearly all the day echoing along the quaintly-fashioned corridors, and bright flowers shedding their perfume in every direction, and joining with the artificial heat in mocking the cold, dreary winter, that reigned without.

My brother's wife loved warmth, and flowers, and music, and meriment, and she had chosen a husband who lived but to provide her with pleasures, and who had ample means wherewith to do it. Of course it followed naturally that Abbeylands offered both to the eye and the senses a scene of luxury such as a prince need not have despised, and opened its hospitable doors to any whose credentials were satisfactory to the fair mistress of the mansion.

But the Christmas guests, with one exception, had all dispersed before I arrived. Walter Kenyon alone remained, to walk, and drive, and sing, and read poetry with Mrs. Guy Beamish, and to give that lady's husband leisure to acquire the tastes and learn the duties of a model country gentleman.

"And how do you think Guy likes all this?" I enquired eagerly of my sister, when, at the close of my second day at Abbeylands, I had an opportunity of speaking to her alone.

"I am a bad watcher, you know, Ethel," Gertrude replied, screening her own pale face as much as possible from my observation; "and Meta is very kind and attentive to me. I don't like, while I am in the house, to speak or even think ill of her."

"It was concerning Guy I questioned you, Gertie. He must see that his wife gives all her time and all her smiles to their guest, while she treats her husband with the sort of condescending indulgence she might exercise towards a child or an animal who was devoted to her. I should have deemed Guy the last man in the world to be satisfied with this style of love from the woman he would sell his soul for."

"Perhaps he is not satisfied," said my sister; "but, seeing no remedy, tries to make the best of it. If we discuss Guy alone, I may acknowledge that I do not think he is happy; but of one thing be assured, Ethel. He would die sooner than be led to utter a word, or breathe a hint of complaint, against Meta."

And this I found to be the case, for walking with him the next morning to one of his farms—he was generally out more than half the day—I tried by every possible means to discover how large the skeleton in his cupboard had grown, and for all my pains I discovered nothing but that he loved his wife more madly and passionately than ever, and would have done battle to the death with anybody who should have presumed to find fault with her.

That Guy disliked and mistrusted Walter Kenyon was, however, abundantly clear, even, I should think, to such an indifferent and

careless watcher as my sister. The two gentlemen never got on well together, never
agreed on any point, and I often fancied that
Meta was amused rather than annoyed at
their antagonism. Perhaps it was owing to
the fact of my mind being a good deal preoccupied with its own cares that I failed
totally in making out how far Walter was
really interested in the seemingly dangerous
game he was playing with my fascinating
sister-in-law. That she did her utmost to win,
not only his passing admiration, but his serious
affection, I am thoroughly convinced—I was
thoroughly convinced of it at the time—but
whether his heart was even temporarily
affected I am quite unable to say. I never
did comprehend that many sided young man,
and I am sure he would have puzzled far
keener observers and far more intelligent
readers of human character than myself.

But Gertrude, bad watcher though she
professed to be, had watched all the colour

out of her cheek, and all the brightness out of her eye, before I joined the party. She never told me anything of herself or her own feelings, but I believed she thought Walter loved Meta, and that the thought was torture to her. It is true that she had shunned him and almost thrust away his affection at the time when he seemed disposed to lay it as an humble offering at her feet; but that she had done this, loving him deeply and truly the while, I had always known, and to witness the danger and degradation of anything we love can never be less than agony.

Walter was far from neglecting my sister even now. I am sure he liked her to be near him, especially when he was reading aloud any of the poets he had taught her to appreciate; but his attentions were not those of a lover, nothing at all resembling those he paid to Meta; and why Gertrude remained to witness so much that made her heart ache I was quite at a loss to imagine. It certainly was not with the faintest design of winning him back to herself; for some reason or other, as yet only dimly guessed at by me, this strange, dear sister of mine, had resolved, from the first, to trample her heart and all its most natural feelings into the dust, to have nothing to do with Walter Kenyon or his love. Perhaps had it been otherwise, had she smiled upon him when her smiles seemed to be the chief object of his ambition, he might have become a wiser and a better man. Who knows? My dear husband always believed that there was a spark of the divine, of the true, and of the good, dwelling somewhere in him, and that it only required favourable circumstances to fan this spark into a flame.

A most difficult and delicate question to handle,—that of the utility or desirability even of such a spark existing in those feeble souls of whom it is mournfully recorded, " Unstable as water they shall not excel!"

The only ray of light thrown upon all this

complicated matter was made visible to me when I had been nearly a week at Abbeylands, under the following circumstances.

Meta announced one morning at breakfast, after reading about half a dozen letters, that Lizzie Vivian was coming to spend a fortnight with her.

"I believe," she added, turning to my sister—"that you, Gertrude, are a greater attraction to the young lady than I am, and perhaps," (glancing slightly to where Walter sat) " that gentleman, who looks so little interested in my intelligence, is a more potent attraction still. Lizzie was always a deep little puss, and I suspect very capable of falling in love without her mamma's leave."

" That was not a nice speech of Meta's in reference to Lizzie Vivian, was it?" I remarked to Gertrude, as she joined me in my room after breakfast.

" No," my sister admitted, " but it was true

nevertheless. I will tell you something of Miss Lizzie, Ethel, if you care to hear it."

Now the truth was Gertie had made the discovery that I, amongst the rest, had some sore trouble on my mind, and with very sisterly tenderness, she did all she could to win my thoughts from dwelling too often on the spectre that haunted them. When I had assured her that I should be interested in anything she had to tell, she took a seat near mine and resumed —

" Part of what I have to relate I discovered accidentally soon after Lizzie came to us, the other part she herself confessed to me in a reckless, passionate mood, when she had ceased to be my pupil, and had called one day at Lindenhurst to repeat the gossip she had heard from her mother on the subject of Walter Kenyon's flirtations with Meta at Brighton."

" Such a child," I observed, " to be mixed up in any way with things of this nature.

Mrs. Vivian must be a most careless mother."

"I fear so. However, the substance of the whole matter is this; Lizzie, according to her own statement, has been fond of Walter ever since she can remember, and her one hope, for the last year at least, has been that he will end by marrying her. By some means or other she found out, while he was staying at Fell House (I fear she must have got at his letters), that instead of being a rich man, as her parents supposed, he was really a very poor one, with only just enough to make a creditable appearance in society— also that to marry a woman with money was his final object, though he was in no hurry to choose a wife at all. Having made this discovery, Miss Lizzie felt tolerably sure of winning her prize in the end, as Walter was aware both of her pecuniary expectations (which are not contemptible) and of her childish partiality for himself. The young lady, however, not quite satisfied with the idea of being taken for her wealth alone, was most anxious to gain the gentleman's favourable opinion, to acquire some influence over him by serving him in little matters, and thus at last secure his affection for herself. It was a half childish, half womanish scheme, and I think it has hitherto been wholly unsuccessful."

As Gertie paused here and began to look less at her ease, to change colour, and to grow restless altogether, I said, with more interest than I had yet felt in the recital :

"And how did the little goose set to work to serve her friend, and to gain the desired influence over him ? "

"Oh," replied my sister, "she did a great number of foolish things, as you may suppose. Amongst the rest, she prevailed on Mrs. Vivian to send her to Lindenhurst, having conceived the idea that Mr. Kenyon admired me, and that if she became the means of his seeing

me or communicating with me, he would
be grateful to her, and it would establish a bond of friendship between them.
She had no fear, you see, knowing Mr.
Kenyon's poverty, of his ever going beyond
what she would have called a flirtation, and
no doubt it struck her that an obscure schoolmistress was a very safe person for her friend
to amuse himself with. I need scarcely tell
you, Ethel, how soon and completely I put a
stop to Miss Lizzie's obliging attempts to act
as a medium between Mr. Kenyon and myself. She had mistaken my character, however adroitly she may have deciphered his.
Of this I know nothing. For Lizzie's sake I
am grieved at his present infatuation, which
no doubt she is coming here with the intention, poor child! of witnessing for herself. I
have no longer much regard for my former
pupil, it is true, but she interested me at first;
she is really but a child still; and I have
some special reasons of my own for believing

that it is Mr. Kenyon's intention finally to marry her."

"Then he must be very worthless, and wholly contemptible!" I said indignantly, "and I am only surprised, Gertie, that you can tolerate him at all, and that Guy does not kick him out of the house."

My sister did not exhibit the least anger or excitement at my fiery words. She only sighed, looking down upon her nervously clenched hands, and said presently :

"Guy is scarcely master in this house, Ethel; and as for my toleration of Mr. Kenyon, I still think less ill of him than you do; and we are all so weak and prone to err when temptation really comes to us."

This from Gertie! Well, I should be surprised at nothing now—but I must just ask her one question.

"And then, dear," I said—"if you wish it, we will have finished with the subject for ever. Tell me whether you think Walter

Kenyon was sincerely attached to you, at the time when we all believed him to be so?"

She was evidently pained at my thus probing her heart, but something had greatly softened her towards me lately, and she answered in a low, almost inaudible voice—

" I think if he had not been a poor man he would have asked me to marry him. And now, dear Ethel, let all that past be a closed book. It is not probable that when I go from Abbeylands I shall ever see him again ; and believe me I never wish to think of him."

Then my sister left me, and after awhile my mind wandered back to my own home and my own sorrows ; and contrasting my beloved and honoured husband with all other men, I felt a passionate desire to kneel at his feet and implore him to forgive my waywardness and jealousy—to take me again to his heart, and love me—just as much and no more than his child's prior claims permitted. These five days' separation from him, these five days' cruel missing of the tender looks and words which, because they had been my heart's daily food I had come to think not rich or sweet enough—had made me very humble—had made me feel that henceforth I should be content to look only at the costly banquet spread for others, and accept for my own portion the crumbs that fell from the rich man's table.

"I must leave you all to-morrow," I announced that day at dinner. "I have had no letters from home since the morning after I arrived, and I am getting anxious."

"Such a model wife!" said my sister-in-law, with her soft, sweet laugh; "I only wonder your husband ever made up his mind to spare you at all."

"If Ethel were not a good wife she would be totally without excuse," remarked my brother warmly, "for there never lived, I am convinced, a better or a worthier man than her husband."

"From my heart I believe it," said Walter Kenyon earnestly; and it was the first and the last time I ever heard him and Guy agree about anything.

As I turned to look at the former more graciously than I was in the habit of doing, I saw, or fancied I saw, in his countenance, something that I always afterwards remembered—something that seemed to tell his life's history, to express a bitter self contempt, mingled with some genuine regret, that while appreciating as he did the beauty of holiness, he was still too weak of purpose, too light of nature to grasp it, and make it his own.

CHAPTER XIII.

THE SPECTRE LAID.

I DID not write to tell them I was returning home a day sooner than I had originally proposed. I thought to give a pleasant surprise, at any rate to some of them—my mother for instance, and old nurse, who had been indignant and vexed at my going away at all. Maggie, too, would doubless be glad to see me; and my husband?—well, I trusted that he would welcome me kindly when he heard how unhappy I had been, and received from my own lips the confession of my foolishness. I meant to tell him everything as soon as I was in his presence again, and bid him punish me in any way that would not entail a further separation between us.

I felt very sad and desolate on arriving at Boltby and finding no one there to meet me. I could not help contrasting this occasion with the one of my return from Devonshire on the bright autumn evening, when Harold and I had walked home over the fields, and been so deliciously happy in our reunion.

"You must never leave me again, my darling!" he had said to me then. And I had confidently replied:

"I never, never will," believing that to go from him voluntarily would always be a simple impossibility.

Fool, fool that I had since been, to trifle with such blessings, such happiness as mine. Oh! did I not deserve to find them wrested from me for ever?

It was much too cold and damp to walk across the fields now—so I took a fly and was driven to Graybourne as quickly as possible. A little more of this miserable desolation of feeling and I should be qualified for admittance into a lunatic asylum, instead of into the peaceful, quiet, home-like vicarage.

Maggie—looking well and almost rosy—was the first I saw after the servant who let me in.

"You, mamma darling?" she cried, opening the parlour door and springing into my arms. "Oh! how nice, how beautiful! I have wanted you every day so much, and I think papa has wanted you too,"—then in a less joyous voice: "Poor papa is not well, but he would go out to-day about something which is a secret. Mrs. Beamish and nurse both asked him not to go. Mrs. Beamish is out too, and Miss Dora is ill and cannot come to see me. Oh! I am so glad—glad—glad— that you have come home; let me give you some more kisses."

Not much to complain of in this welcome at any rate.

"But now tell me, love, what is the matter with papa?" I said, when we were both seated by the blazing fire, Maggie at my feet and I in the dear old-fashioned easy chair which I claimed as my own, because before he married me it had always been my husband's—"he is not very unwell, I hope?"

"Not ill, you know, as I was," she replied, gravely; "but nurse says he is not at all 'the thing,' and when she says that of people she means they are not well; besides, papa looks white and does not eat much, and doesn't laugh like he does when you are with him. I tell you what, mamma," (and the little voice grew quite mysterious and confidential), "I believe he has been unhappy because you went way. You won't go away again without taking papa and me with you, will you?"

I said: "No, my darling," and very certainly I meant it; but I spoke absently, for the child had made me terribly uneasy, and all my thoughts revolved round this new subject of my husband's illness.

"I must go and get my things off and my dress changed," I said to Maggie presently, "and in the meanwhile you shall order up the tea, and by the time papa comes in we shall all be ready for it."

But I stole from the parlour into my husband's study and sat waiting there, in very miserable suspense and anxiety, till he should return home.

The half hour that I waited seemed an age to me, for I had worked myself up to such a pitch of nervousness that I expected nothing less than to find that my Harold was dying, and that my repentance and desire to atone had come too late.

When the hall door opened and shut, my heart began to beat so violently that I thought I must suffocate. Then came the firm, rather slow tread, along the passage, then the hand on the study door, finally the latch of that door lifted, and we two face to face.

Whether I sprang to him or whether he came to me, I cannot tell. I remember nothing prior to that long, clinging, tender embrace, in which he held me, and in which my very heart seemed sinking and failing from its excess of gladness and delight. Only to be with him again ; only to feel his arms around me ; only to know that I was still dear to him ; this was a feast, after my late starvation, that I thought I could never make enough of.

But when he put me at length a little away from him, and looked with those kind, kind eyes, into my face, and said:

" My wife, are you better ?"

The long pent up tears rushed forth, and I slid down to his feet and told him all.

If he had known or guessed my folly before he kept his own counsel, or the counsel, of those who had enlightened him, well.   He listened patiently to my confession, sometimes during its progress stroking my hair, or drawing my trembling hands fondly into his own, but he did not once interrupt me till I had quite finished, and then he raised me up —I would not let him lift me sooner—to a seat beside him, and told me I must hear *his* story now.

" It shall be shorter than yours, Ethel," he said, with a tender smile that fell like dew upon my heart, " and yet not altogether dissimilar. Child, you have been yearning for more love from me—not knowing that the measure I gave was so abundant and overflowing that I recognized its excess as sin, as a robbery at least of Him who had said to me, 'my son, give me thine heart!' My Ethel, you never had a rival nor the shadow of a rival in my affection. A hundred daughters, each of them as dear as Maggie, and she is very dear to me, would have counted as less than nothing in my estimation in comparison with you, my wife, my heart's darling! But as soon as I discovered the extent of the love you had inspired, I became possessed with the idea that God would judge me for my idolatry—that he would take either Maggie or yourself away from me. When Maggie's first illness came on I trembled, and thought, in my blindness, that I might avert the punishment I dreaded and had merited, by striving to love my idol less —by denying myself at least the dear delight of your constant presence, the joy of showing you every instant how dear you were, and of reading in your innocent eyes that my love was your happiness. Ah, child—child —I may tell you in words, but you will never quite understand, what you are to me, nor what I have suffered in struggling to make you less. With Maggie's recovery my fears were lulled to sleep, and except during your own short illness at Ventnor, when you know

I scarcely breathed away from you, all went on smoothly until this last affair which has been so severe a trial to us both. Had Maggie died, I should have believed that God had thus punished me for my too entire devotedness to my wife, but even this would not have diminished the love that once given I have no power to recal. Ethel, our child has been mercifully spared. God has been very good to us. We both owe to Him, at least the earnest wish, the constant prayer, that by His grace we may be enabled to love Him first and best, and each other in and after Him. Will my darling join with me in wishing and praying thus ?"

But I had no voice; I had no words: I could only sit in a dream of ineffable content-ment, clasping my husband's hands, gazing into his face, and thinking it quite impossible that with this newly acquired certainty of his precious love, I could ever experience a care or a sorrow again.

When at length we joined my mother and Maggie at tea, the latter exclaimed triumphantly that papa was looking quite well now, and that she knew all along he had only wanted mamma to make him so.

"But you frightened me very much about papa's illness, Maggie,"I said, observing, now the excitement of meeting me was over, that Harold did look thinner than usual. "As it is, I see I shall have to take him in hand. Perhaps he has not had his long walks lately."

"I expect he has had a tolerably long one to-day," remarked my mother, with a reproving shake of the head at her son-in-law; "but if Ethel does not know yet, don't let me betray the secret."

"Oh, to be sure," I said, looking from one to the other and detecting smiles on all their faces. "Maggie told me something about a secret which had taken this obstinate gentleman out against your better judgment to-day. Please one of you enlighten me quickly, for I am tingling all over with curiosity."

My husband only imprisoned my hand in his own, and left mamma to explain—

"Well, the truth is," she continued, "the vicar has been fancying since you left home that you are not so strong as you were, or so capable of taking long walks. He heard of a little carriage and pony to be sold at some place beyond Boltby, and having been once to look at it, he walked over to conclude the bargain this afternoon, meaning to meet you at the coach with it to-morrow. You have just come home a day too soon, my dear."

I was too deeply touched at this great, great kindness and thoughtfulness, at a time when I so ill-deserved anything of the sort, to be able to do more than look my fervent thanks, while Maggie expatiated on the joys of pony carriages in general, and of this one that had become our own in particular. But, as we were all leaving the table, I whispered to my husband—

"Dearest Harold, you are far, far too good, to your unworthy wife; but do you say with mamma that I have come home a day too soon?"

"I will not tell you my opinion on that subject," he replied, laughing and kissing me, "for you are the greediest little woman in the matter of love that the world has ever known, and have urgent need of severe correction and discipline. Come and sit with me, however, in my study to-night, and to-morrow we will begin to be a sensible, rational, well behaved couple—something quite different from what we have been hitherto."

"Ah, you cannot frighten me now," I said, clinging joyfully to the dear hand that was leading me on. "I have got at a more important secret this evening than the secret of the pony carriage, and you may be sure I shall be woman enough to make it serve my own ends."

"I think I may trust you, my darling," was his loving answer; "since all I require of you is that henceforth, to the close of our joint lives, you will fully and entirely trust *me.*"

CHAPTER XIV.

MARRYING AND GIVING IN MARRIAGE.

In the June of that year two events occurred which excited almost equal interest in our very quiet village. The first was the arrival of a little stranger of the male sex at the vicarage, who bid fair to give his mother enough work to guarantee her against all visionary fancies of every description in the future, and who certainly soon became quite as formidable a rival of herself in the vicar's affections as Maggie had ever been.

M 2

The second event was the marriage of Jane Norton to the excellent Mr. Burns. As my little boy was only three weeks old when the wedding took place I was unable to attend personally, but my husband gave me a tolerably graphic account of the whole affair, and the details, which, as a man, he naturally omitted, were supplied by my sister and Mrs. Arnott.

"Of course," explained the last-named lady, when she just dropped in to see me and my baby, after the breakfast at the cottage—" of course the bride looked absurdly young, for such an elderly man as Mr. Burns, though he was very well ' got up ' for the occasion, and might really have passed for thirty-five. Jane had a pretty white silk bonnet on, and a really handsome veil that I suspect Mr. B— must have given her, but if I had been her aunts I would have dressed her in something a little less juvenile than plain white muslin. A good rich silk, or poplin, now, would have made the disparity of years seem less. After all, however, she has been a fortunate girl, for of course she will have her own way in everything, and I know Mr. Burns has money over and above what he makes by his editorship. By the bye, Miss Harriet has quite left off writing verses for his paper. I have not seen the signature of 'Semiramis' for months, in the poet's corner. Poor dear lady! there has certainly come a change over the spirit of her dream, but I know you don't approve of gossip now that you are the vicar's wife. Oh, and speaking of clergymen, have you had any news of that dear Mr. Leslie since I saw you?"

So she rattled on, believing no doubt that she was making herself exceedingly agreeable, but really tiring me a good deal, and forcing me at last to the inhospitality of telling her that I was prohibited at present from listening to much talking.

My husband came in to sit with me and to

refresh my spirit after the widow's exit, but although he too spoke chiefly of Jane, and her apparently happy prospects, the train of thought into which I was led on being left alone again, passed over my young friend and the comfortable destiny she had, without any effort, secured, and alighted on the hearth of a certain little room in her late home, where, in imagination, I saw Miss Harriet Downing sitting that bright wedding morning alone, and with her face-mask laid down beside her

Sitting and looking steadfastly at last at the shape and fashion of that hope which not so long ago had arisen like a glowing sun upon the horizon of her life, to shine on her and warm her for a little space, to dazzle her eyes with visions of a beautiful dream world, and then suddenly to sink down deep, deep behind the clouds, leaving her—as it would seem at first—in perpetual darkness.

But she is a strong, brave, unselfish woman,

not only willing to look boldly at her folly, but to strike at it with her own firm hand, to heap upon it her own self loathing, to trample it in the dust which her tears shall make clay of, to bury it out of sight for ever. And so she sits alone on Jane's wedding morning, with the face-mask that she will need to wear no more, thrown off, and contemplating it nearly with the same disdain that the weakness which suggested its use has inspired. But she will rise up presently and resume all the quiet duties of her life with a placid smile and kinder, gentler words, for all around her, that she has gone through this personal sorrow, and tasted, at least once, the bitterness of a heart left desolate.

As Jane Norton, or rather, Mrs. Burns, will not come into this story again, I may mention here that she never showed any symptoms of regretting her early marriage, or of being dissatisfied with her kind and indulgent, though certainly elderly husband.

He allowed her to fill their house with dumb pets of every description, and even when more intelligent ones arrived the first favourites were not discarded, but continued to share with the white-frocked little angels the attention and caresses of the girl matron who, as a wife and mother, became nearly as busy and industrious as she had formerly been the reverse.

Owing to the distance between our homes, and the multiplicity of our respective duties, Jane and myself did not meet very often after her marriage ; but whenever I could contrive to get as far as her house in that famous little pony carriage the reader has heard of, I was quite certain of a very cordial welcome, which might, perhaps, have been more agreeable had it not always been vociferously echoed by dogs, parrots, canaries, cats, and babies, who during the whole day seemed to make their noise in concert in the poor editor's dwelling.

As my own domestic cares and anxieties

increased, my dear sister became my constant companion and helper. She could never complain now that she had not enough work to do, or that her life was useless to others, and yet I could not shut my eyes to the fact that Gertie was really an unhappy and a disappointed woman. I believe it is only given to a very few of our sex to content themselves with duties in which they are not the prime agents or directors. We do hear occasionally of spinster aunts and cousins throwing all their hearts and souls into labours which are scarcely recognized as theirs, and which never bring them anything to speak of either in the way of thanks or credit. But I am sure the majority of women, to work cheerfully and successfully, require a field in which they can be the generals, and duties which their own minds and hands can shape out as well as perform.

My dear sister was one of these women, and, therefore, all that I gave her to do and

really thanked her for doing, while it employed her time, failed totally in interesting
her heart.　If it had not been for mamma's
strong objection, I do believe she would have
attempted a school again, and I am quite sure
she often wished Mr. King's legacy at the
bottom of the sea.　It had brought her no
more real satisfaction, if less positive misfortune, than it had brought to Guy.

Before the expiration of my brother's second
year at Abbeylands, Meta's reckless extrava-
gance had obliged him to sell the whole property and to go abroad to retrench.　We saw
them both prior to their leaving England, as
they came, at mamma's earnest entreaty, to
spend a fortnight at Lindenhurst.　We all
thought Guy much changed; he looked ill in
body, and very sick in mind, though while
with us it was evident that he made super-
human efforts to conceal the grief that was
preying upon him and turning his life's cup
into gall.　My dear husband had said that he

would, sooner or later, reap the whirlwind, but I never thought his reaping day would begin so early as this.

As for Meta, she looked, when her rouge was off, at least ten years older, and her spirits were very fitful and uncertain, sometimes raising her to the heights of childish animation and gaiety, but oftener plunging her into depths of gloom and even sullenness that no one could venture to meddle with. The most vigilant observer amongst us failed in detecting any open unkindness on her part towards Guy. She always appeared to consider him as an innocent and unoffending appendage to herself, whom it would be bad taste and waste of time to quarrel with. In some of her moods she would certainly indulge in a little ill-natured sarcasm on the subject of Guy's failure in his agricultural projects, but he never reminded her that she had squandered the money that might have enabled him to carry them out, nor that but for her imperious will, or whim, he would have been engaged in duties and pursuits infinitely more congenial to his natural tastes than those connected with farms and the breeding of cattle. I am quite sure the remembrance of what he had given up to please Meta, the thought of all his gifts and talents unemployed and useless, weighed upon his mind as frequently, if not as bitterly, as his disappoint-ment in Meta herself; a disappointment which after all we only assumed, since never, by word or conscious look, did my brother even yet depreciate his idol.

Their visit was not productive of much enjoyment to any of us, and an event occurred just at the end of it which left a heavier dread on my mind as well as on my husband's—(I spoke of it to no one else)—than I had till now allowed myself to cherish in reference to my brother's future.

Harold and myself were dining one evening at Lindenhurst, and Mrs. Arnott had been invited, in honour of Meta, to come in to tea. We were remarking that the fair widow was later than it was her custom to be on such occasions, when suddenly she presented herself, in a state of immense excitement, and gasping out the overwhelming intelligence— (overwhelming to some of us)—that Lizzie Vivian had that morning eloped from her mother's house—eloped with Walter Kenyon.

"I can tell you all about it," continued this unrivalled retailer of gossip and scandal, "for my cousin has only lately been on a visit at Fell House, and of course Mrs. Vivian let her, as an old friend, into the family secrets. It appears that Miss Lizzie, who is not yet eighteen, has long set her heart upon marrying this fascinating young gentleman, and until Mr. and Mrs. V—— discovered that, like the pretty milkmaid, his face was his fortune, they were not at all averse to the match. Naturally, when they did find out that little fact, they peremptorily forbade the banns, and requested Mr. Walter to quit their hospitable mansion for a season. He obeyed them like a courteous gentleman as he is, but he took Miss Lizzie's heart and promises away with him, and the result is the charming little escapade of this morning. I understand that the parents are furious, as they may well be, since Lizzie's money is quite independent of them, and she can touch it on arriving at the age of nineteen."

While Mrs. Arnott was speaking, we had all turned our faces naturally in her direction, but as soon as she came to a full stop, waiting, I presume, for our comments, I looked round to where my sister and Meta were sitting, side by side, and there was something that struck me in both their countenances. Gertie, who had a little knowledge of the difficult art of self-control, had only grown a shade paler than usual, and exhibited with this paleness the kind of aspect a tender-hearted angel might assume on hearing of the sudden downfall of a weak, frail mortal. But Meta's expression was of a very different nature, and though I scarcely did more than glance at her, I was really startled and alarmed; she looked so wrathful, so vindictive, so bitterly disdainful, and withal so piteously miserable, that had the occasion been other than it was, or seemed to be, I could not have chosen but pitied her.

Mamma and Guy, and even my husband, had in the meanwhile each spoken, offering some remark or asking some question in connection with Mrs. Arnott's information, and now that voluble lady was going on again, was expatiating on Lizzie's cleverness in outwitting her parents, was conjecturing as to how the young couple would manage to live until the wife's fortune fell in, was ringing all the changes, in her own peculiarly flippant style, on the relishing and apparently unwearying subject, when suddenly I missed Meta from the room. I had not seen her go.

I had not heard the door open. I turned presently to Guy, and asked him carelessly, what had become of his wife.

"She went out ten minutes ago," he said, and something quite forlorn in the tone of his voice went to my heart, and steeled it more than ever against Meta.

Still speaking carelessly, and as if I had no particular interest in his answer, I next enquired whether they had seen much of Walter Kenyon at Abbeylands lately, or met him in London or elsewhere.

"Oh, pretty well," Guy replied, and I thought absently, for his eyes were continually turned towards the door. "Idle young men, you know, are glad of a house like ours, where they can come and stay whenever it suits them, and this Walter, it appears, was quite a lady's man; he amused Meta."

Amused Meta! I scarcely think this last achievement of his had amused her very much.

It was quite half an hour before she came into the room again, and what I discovered then I revealed to my husband (because I never kept anything from him, and it was a relief to my own burdened mind to speak), as we walked home from Lindenhurst that evening.

"Harold," I said, "did you notice what wild spirits Guy's wife was in all the latter part of the evening; how she talked, and with what animation she sang, and how captivating altogether she became?"

"I noticed certainly that she seemed much livelier than usual," he replied, "but you know, Ethel dear, I neither like nor admire this sister-in-law of yours. Guy's face, as I have seen it sometimes lately, quite haunts me."

"Ah, poor Guy! but I want to tell you of a discovery I have made to-night, Harold. It will shock you very much, I am sure, but I am right in my conclusion. I have not a doubt about it. Meta drinks!"

He said so quietly—"You think so, do
you?" that it was my turn to be astonished.
I was going to ask him if he did not consider it very dreadful, when, quite as quietly
as before, he continued:—

"I have known this, my darling, ever
since they have been here. I found it out
immediately. Her fitful spirits, her strange
ways at times, her invariable habit of going
up to her own room for some portion of the
evening, and above all, Guy's evident broken
heartedness, have formed altogether a chain
of reasons for arriving at this one terrible conclusion that have left little to my penetration
in the matter. I should not have spoken of
it to you, had you not discovered it for yourself, and in case your mother and sister should
be still in ignorance, I recommend you not to
enlighten them. There is no vice that so
completely shuts out hope for those who have
once taken to it as this. God help and comfort your poor brother, for he is indeed to be
pitied."

I did not on that occasion say anything to my husband about Walter Kenyon, and the strange emotion Meta had betrayed on hearing of his marriage to Lizzie, but I thought of it all with very deep anxiety, and when I came at last to bid farewell to Guy, a terrible foreboding mingled with the sisterly blessings I was invoking upon him, and like a death knell in my ears rang out those solemn words :

" They have sown the wind. They shall reap the whirlwind."

CHAPTER XV.

WALTER'S WIFE.

THE only events of importance that occurred
during the next year were the return of
Edmund Hallam to take possession of his
title and estate, and Alicia Clarkson's marriage to him. That dear girl had said when
he first sinned against her that she could not
forgive him because she had never been angry
with him, but by whatever name she desig-
nated the clemency he required, she must

have bestowed it as soon as he came to sue for it, inasmuch as the wedding took place at Beechwood immediately after his arrival there; and once more the venerable lady of the mansion threw open her hospitable gates and assembled her friends and neighbours around her.

Gertrude went with our party—that is with my husband, Maggie, and myself—the two little ones in the nursery not being quite of an age to mingle in such gaieties. My dear sister had tried hard to get out of accepting Mrs. Hallam's invitation, but we all believed it would do her good, and so she had given in at last and taken the fourth seat in our carriage. I could not help looking at her that day, and thinking how beautiful she still was, and when I say "still" was, I do not refer to the few years that had elapsed since I first described her as very fair to look upon, but to the cares and anxieties and disappointments which she had experienced, either on her own or others' behalf, and which things I am inclined to believe do, in a general way, far more towards destroying beauty than even that arch destroyer, Time himself.

But Gertrude's loveliness was not of the kind which easily fades—not the mere freshness and beauty of early youth that every year must take something from, but rather the less common charm of perfect features united to an expression of thoughtful intelligence which neither time nor sorrow could greatly interfere with.

And it was not my sisterly partiality that made me deem her lovely still, for when Mrs. Hallam was speaking to our party she singled out Gertrude, as she had done on that former occasion more than three years ago, and asked her smilingly what had come to all the chivalry of England that so fair a flower was still blooming alone.

Very red was the rose that bloomed on my sister's pale cheek as the old lady thus condescendingly jested with her, and not quite so steady or self-possessed as usual was her voice as she replied:

" There should be one unmarried in every family, Mrs. Hallam, and I am more than content to be that one in ours."

So she passed on. And I remarked to Harold afterwards that Gertie had less appreciation of compliments, less personal vanity, than any woman, plain or handsome, that I had ever known.

" She is not a weak woman by any means," he said—" and this you know, Ethel, was one of the reasons why I used to think she would have made such a good wife for poor Walter. By the bye, if I see Mrs. Vivian to-day, I will ask her about Lizzie and her husband ; nobody ever seems to hear a word of them."

We did see Mrs. Vivian in the course of the morning, and in reply to my husband's enquiries (I don't think anybody else would have ventured to make them), she told us that the Kenyons were somewhere on the continent, living recklessly she supposed, on the paltry sum which had formed the principal of Walter's very insignificant income. " They know," she added bitterly, "that Lizzie must come in for her money when she is nineteen; and so they are no doubt spending all the little they have got at present, with perfect unconcern.   Mr. Vivian is willing to receive and forgive them, but for my part, I never will."

Poor woman! she might have felt and spoken differently had she been able to look on a little way into the future; for the next news we had of the unforgiven child—three months later—was of a very mournful kind; and no doubt when it came to the angry mother, she remembered those words: "Vengeance is mine.   I will repay, saith the Lord."

To me this sad intelligence concerning Lizzie Kenyon was conveyed in a letter from the Countess of Clinton, who had since her marriage been travelling with her husband through France and Italy. From a small town in the latter country she wrote:—

" You will, I know, dear Ethel, be interested in the melancholy news I have to send you of an old friend whom, quite accidentally, I discovered here about a week ago—Lizzie Vivian that was. When Edmund and myself met her in the public gardens one evening, she was accompanied by her husband, Mr. Kenyon, and they both appeared very well, and very gay. Lizzie told me they had been living at this place for four or five months, that it was pretty and cheap, and that they both liked it. She further informed me, when the two gentlemen had walked a little apart from us, that she expected very soon to become a mother, and that she was delighted with the prospect—also that her husband was excessively good to her, and that she should be quite happy if only her parents would forgive and receive her. I called upon her the next day, and then they came and dined with us.

After this we met two or three times every day, and still Lizzie appeared in excellent health and spirits, and Mr. Kenyon always most kind and attentive to her. It did not strike me that he was as much in love with his young wife as she was with him; but this may have been my fancy, and at any rate Lizzie was perfectly content. Two days ago. I called early, by appointment, at their lodgings, to take the wife for a drive in the country, Judge, dear Ethel, of the frightful shock I received, when the portress of the house informed me, in an awe-stricken voice, that the poor young lady had been delivered of a still-born child an hour ago, and had since died. The husband, she said, had been locked in the room with his dead wife and child, ever since the physician had left; and he would admit nobody. I immediately drove home and sent Edmund to see what he could do. After awhile poor Mr. Kenyon admitted him, and finally came home to our hotel, and is with us now. I am quite sure, whatever may have been his sentiments towards his wife, he feels her sudden death most dreadfully, and this quite apart from the sad position in which it leaves him, as Lizzie, not being nineteen, had not received a penny of her large fortune, the whole of which can now be claimed by her parents, for the other children. Mr. Kenyon told Edmund, that he had now no resource in the world but his talent as an artist. We shall do what we can to help him a little, delicately, but until the funeral is over no plans as to the future can be even hinted at. Poor Lizzie and her baby will be buried the day after to-morrow. I cannot write on any other subject yet," &c., &c., &c.

And " poor Lizzie!" I echoed through the blinding tears which had rained down on Alicia's letter. Alas! she had doubtless remembered many of the accomplishments, many of the graces which since her child-hood she had been taught; but she had for-gotten, when its remembrance might have availed her, one of the earliest lessons she must have learned at her nurse's or her mother's knee.

"Honour thy father and thy mother, *that thy days may be long in the land* which the Lord thy God giveth thee!"

CHAPTER XVI.

META'S DOOM.

FROM the time of my brother's leaving
England with his wife, we were kept very
much in the dark concerning all that was
happening to them.   A brief letter from Guy
about once in three months, with occasionally
a line or two added by Meta, was the extent
of what we received, and these communications were usually of the vaguest and most
unsatisfactory description.   Either the
travellers were just arriving at a place, or
just leaving it, or Meta was sick, or Guy was
not in a writing mood, or something or other

had occurred to form an excuse for his very short and constrained letters. Once, soon after Lizzie Kenyon's death, my brother thus alluded to Walter. " We stumbled the other day at Rome upon an old acquaintance who is living there now, in a very humble way, and studying painting as a profession. You will have guessed that it was Walter Kenyon, whose wife, you know, died so suddenly about three months ago. Lord and Lady Clinton have been very kind to him, but he is an independent fellow, and will not receive obligations unless he can be made to believe that he is the obliging party. We asked him to come and see us—Meta thought it would be a change for him, but beyond leaving his card he did not avail himself of our invitation, and as my wife's health is very bad I would not press the point. He looks ill, and I fancy the circumstances attending poor Mrs. Kenyon's death have left a deep impression on his mind. He was no favourite of mine formerly, but from the little I have seen of him now I should judge him to be greatly improved. The school of adversity turns out, occasionally, some very noble characters."

This letter was addressed to me, but I showed it to Gertrude, who returned it without a single comment—only I knew by something in her face then, and for days after, that the lonely widower toiling for his bread in Rome was not unpitied or unthought of, at least by one friend, in England.

Another winter and spring went by and then my brother's letters began to be more frequent. Meta was very ill, was growing worse; every new change of place seemed only to increase her illness. Guy did not mention of what nature it was—he wrote as under the influence of extreme mental anguish, sometimes as if he scarcely knew what he said, never as if he entertained any hope either for himself or his wife in the future. We all felt for him deeply—he was our constant subject of thought and conversation. Poor mamma was quite heart-broken in reflecting on the miserable destiny of her favourite child; she wrote and implored him to bring Meta home if she could by any means bear the journey, but no answer came to this letter, and for more than a month we endured a martyrdom of suspense and anxiety.

Alas! when that was ended we would gladly have returned to the doubt and the uncertainty again.

It was early in September—I cannot forget the time, because my husband, my children (I had three now, besides Maggie), and myself, had been celebrating baby's birthday—baby, of course, being present in her nurse's arms — by drinking tea under the walnut tree mentioned before in this story. We had just finished our little meal, and Maggie—a handsome girl now of about thirteen—had taken my two pets, the youngest of whom could just toddle, to gather fruit, while baby and nurse had been sent in out of the evening air, when Harold and myself were startled by the appearance of a stranger advancing rather quickly towards us from the paddock side of the garden.   Now as the gate opening into the paddock, though not always locked, was never used, except by the family, it was natural that we should be surprised at seeing that a strange gentleman had passed through it without permission, and quite as if he had a right to take the liberty.

When we first saw him he had but just come through the gate, and some intervening trees shielded him for a few seconds after this from our closer observation.   But presently he was upon the lawn fronting us, and then with a sudden cry I started up, exclaiming:—

" Harold, it is Guy, my brother !"

" Nonsense, child!" he replied, half amused and half anxious at my vehemence, and trying to draw me down to my seat again; " it is no more like Guy than I am.   Some poor young man who has fallen sick, perhaps, in passing through the village, and wants to see me.   He looks fearfully ill, Ethel."

"But it is Guy, or his ghost," I repeated, as the object of our discussion came nearer; and then I broke away from my unbelieving husband and rushed to meet the shadowy figure on the lawn, to clasp it in my arms, whether it was of flesh and blood or of unsubstantial air, and to sob over it as if my tears were to decide the matter.

"Ethel," spoke out the figure; "I can afford you no time now for grieving over me; all that may be done later. Now I want you to come with me to my dying wife. I was bringing her home by the slowest and easiest stages when about fifteen miles from this she broke down utterly. I have left her at a poor man's cottage on the road, where these last fatal symptoms seized her. I sent back a doctor from the nearest town I came to after that. I would not have left her but that she implored me so frantically to come and fetch you; and the woman into whose charge I gave her seemed kind and motherly. I took fresh horses at Boltby, and the carriage is waiting for us on the other side of your field. Can you come at once?"

By this time Harold had joined us on the lawn, and his strong arm had lent me the support I really needed in going through this strange and agitating meeting with my unhappy brother. I trembled so much that it was my husband who first answered for me.

" Ethel shall get ready immediately, Guy, but she is a little overcome, you see, by your abrupt appearance, and by the great change in yourself. You will have a glass of wine while your sister is making her preparations. Come with me to my study where we shall be quiet and alone. These are sad, sad tidings, you have brought us."

Now that poor Guy had delivered his errand, and ascertained that no opposition would be made to my accompanying him to Meta, his strength and energy appeared all to desert him; a dull, hopeless, resigned expression, came into his worn face, and he suffered himself to be led, unresisting, into the house.

In the meanwhile I ran about like a person possessed, giving a hundred directions here and there, kissing again and again the astonished and half-frightened children, imploring Maggie not to lose sight of them in my absence, scrambling together a few necessary articles of clothing, and finally, with a very heavy and reluctant heart (for it was a serious trial to me to be torn so abruptly from my home and all my beloved ones), returning to Guy, and announcing my readiness to set forth with him.

" God bless and support you, my darling," whispered Harold, as he held me in his arms, at parting. " You have doubtless a most painful scene before you, but my Ethel knows where to look for strength, and she knows, too, that her husband's heart and prayers will be with her."

" And you will take care of our darlings ?"

I said, choking down my weak tears, and clinging for a moment to my children's father as if he could give me the courage needed. "I have never left them before, you know, Harold."

From the time Guy and myself entered the carriage until we left it again—and I think we must have been quite two hours on the road—we did not exchange half-a-dozen sentences. I saw that he was not only unwilling to talk, but actually incapable of doing so. I could only dimly conjecture then, or at any future period, what had been the exact nature of the sufferings of those last three years; but judging from their terrible effects on my brother's mind, I am sure they must have been in themselves terrible.

It was dark when we arrived at the cottage, and the woman who received us at the door, and who informed Guy that the poor lady seemed a bit easier since she had taken something the doctor had sent her, lighted us up into Meta's room by the aid of a dim tallow candle, which she deposited on a small, ricketty table, by the bed, telling us she had sent to the town, and we should have a better light presently.

Then she left us, closing the door after her; and Guy, throwing himself into one of the miserable chairs, signed for me to take off my bonnet, and to make known my arrival to his wife.

"Is she not asleep?" I whispered, after I had given one glance at the white, emaciated form, stretched on that humble bed.

"No," he said, "she scarcely ever sleeps, poor girl! When her frightful attacks are over, she generally lays in the sort of stupor she is in now for an hour or two; but she will rouse up if you speak to her."

So I nerved my sinking spirit as well as I could, and going close to the bed, laid my hand on the shadowy hand of its occupant.

"Meta, dear, I have come to see you. Guy has brought me. Are you able to say a word to me?"

Then she opened her languid eyes—something new and strange in their expression made me recoil from her for a moment—and replied faintly, and in a hollow tone:

"Thank you for coming. I will speak presently. Guy knows what to give me."

I turned to my brother, and saw that, in addition to the look of unutterable anguish in his face, there appeared in it, as his wife's last words reached his ear, an expression of disgust, of shrinking horror, that, though I partially understood it, I was deeply pained to witness.

If the idol his very soul had worshipped had become, through her own degrading vice, loathsome in his sight, then indeed I could enter into the exceeding bitterness of the woe that was consuming him.

"The doctor has probably left you a restorative, Meta," he replied, getting up and looking about the room. "You have already taken something," he said, "have you not?"

"Yes; but it was only a foolish sedative,

and if I am to gain strength for talking, I must have a stimulant of some kind. What does it matter now, Guy?" she continued, in a tone so plaintive and despairing that it went to my heart; "the end must come as swiftly and as surely whether I am denied this last little help or indulged in it. I want to talk to your sister; you have brought her here on purpose. Do, do, Guy, give me some brandy."

Oh, how I pitied the wretched husband at that moment when, with his white, sunken cheek glowing with burning shame, and with his eyes cast to the earth, that I, his sister, might not see the revolted look that was in them, he caught up a bottle and glass that appeared to have been hidden behind the curtain, and poured out a small quantity (adding water to it) of the pale liquid the bottle contained.

" Bah, it is not enough," said Meta, complainingly; but, as he took no notice of this, she drank it off quickly, fiercely, greedily,

and then, handing him back the glass,
said:

"You may leave us now, my poor Guy.
A change from this wretched room will do
you good. Take a walk in the fresh, night
air which *I* shall never breathe again, and so
its breath henceforth will come sweeter and
purer to you. The doctor will be here again
in an hour. No use, no use; but he can try
his best, and you will be satisfied."

I think Guy was gone before she had quite
done speaking to him. His breaking heart
panted no doubt for some freer atmosphere,
some larger space, some unpeopled ground on
which to sob out its agony—and he did not
know, he could not guess, that the end Meta
had alluded to was so very near.

"We are alone now, then," she said, nervously clutching and holding fast my
hand when she perceived that her husband
had left us—" and I may try what the confession of my past sins and wickedness will
do towards relieving the intolerable burden

that is at present resting on my soul. I have chosen you, Ethel, to receive this confession, not because amongst your family I like you the best, but because you have already gained a more intimate knowledge of me than the others. You have always known me to be weak and selfish and wayward—perhaps you have judged me to be criminal?"

As this last clause was in the form of a question, and Meta was waiting for me to answer it, I said, reluctantly:

"I have certainly not had a good opinion of you since you became my brother's wife. When I was with you at Abbeylands your conduct greatly shocked and displeased me."

I think, but the candle burning so dimly I could not be sure, that there came a hectic flush upon Meta's faded cheeks as I said this. I know the hand that was holding mine shook more than it had yet done, as she continued—

"But I have never been what the world calls criminal, Ethel. I swear it to you now on my dying bed. I tried to make Walter Kenyon love me. I wanted his love because it seemed difficult to win. He flirted with me and gratified his own vanity, but he cared no more for me than he did for you. If he ever cared for anybody, which I doubt, it was that cold, beautiful Gertrude. You would perhaps enquire why I, married to a man who doated on me, should have sought another man's love at all. This comes into the mystery I once promised to reveal to you of my strange and unfortunate nature. Throughout my woman's life—and I think I was a woman at fifteen—I have been possessed of a demon—a devil if you will—continually urging me to gain all the love I could, and making it, when gained, utterly valueless to me. You will call it vanity. I have never so considered it. Vanity gives nothing in exchange for what it gets—I gave my own love fully and freely, until I was quite sure of possessing that which I sought. Then—and how could I help this?—my heart seemed to

turn to ice.   I had obtained the object of my
passionate craving ; I held it in my hand—it
was my own, and the question ever came
Qu'en ferai-je?   I did not want it, for my
own love was at an end, and the interest of my
life—for the time being—at an end too.
Walter Kenyon was the only man whose affection I ever sought and failed to win.   This
maddened me ; this intensified my own feelings towards him (I see by your face that you
think I desecrate the word 'love' by applying
it to such unhallowed sentiments as mine),
but this coldness on his part, I repeat, intensified my feelings, till they became torture to me
—a torture my undisciplined heart refused to
bear.   Then began the craving for artificial
excitement, the thirst for stimulants which has
destroyed my life, and alas ! I fear the life of
my poor patient Guy as well.   Ethel, my
death will be the only good thing he has ever
received at my hands, the only return I shall
ever have made him for all his past devoted
love and tenderness.   It is an awful thought

on a death-bed—the thought of having blighted the whole existence of a fellow mortal —and I have many other awful thoughts beside this to contend with. I am a very pitiful, wretched creature, Ethel, dying without even the satisfaction of feeling that I have ever enjoyed the mess of pottage, for which I have sold my soul. Everything that I have grasped at, because it has seemed fair and lovely in my sight, has turned into a heap of dust and ashes in my hand; and that which might have kept its form and beauty, and blessed me and purified my heart, I have spurned as if it were nothing worth, trampled upon it till not a fraction of its original shape has remained. So with my husband's love, Ethel; but come closer to me, let me speak this in your ear— Guy abhors me, loathes me, shrinks from me, as though I were some vile and polluted thing. He does not know that I have found this out; he has tried very hard to conceal it; his treatment of me has been as gentle, as kind, as considerate as if he loved me still. Poor tender-hearted, sensitive Guy ! what a life it has been for him.   But he will be avenged, Ethel.   He is avenged even now. The unutterable horrors of the dark, lonely grave are coming upon me thick and fast. I am dying hopeless, wretched, unforgiven.   I am —"

Here something in her voice seemed to choke her, and her eyes every minute grew wilder and more fearful to look upon.   A great dread had seized me that she would die while I was there alone with her, and before I could summon courage or strength (for all the agitation I had undergone had made me weaker than an infant), to speak to her of the Redeemer, who, even at this eleventh hour, could pardon and bless her guilty soul.

At that first pause which exhaustion caused her to make, I took both her cold hands in mine ; I compelled myself to look steadfastly into those burning, terrible eyes, and I said in a low but distinct voice :

" Meta, do you wish to have your sins forgiven, to be reconciled to your offended God, to join the countless multitude who are now praising Him for unmerited grace and mercy, in Heaven?"

"Do not mock me," she cried, with something of the old fierceness lending momentary strength to her voice—"I might wish for annihilation if I could believe in it—but all other wishes are over for me. Do not usurp your husband's province, Ethel, and preach to a lost creature like myself. You mean well; you are fulfilling your duty; but as far as my benefit is concerned it is too late, too late! Let me die in peace."

"Dear Meta, it is peace I am anxious to bring to you," I said, again stooping down and kissing her in the forlorn hope that some human feeling entering into her poor heart might pave the way for a ray of divine light; "the peace of God that you may even yet attain if you will trust wholly in His goodness. Meta, you have yearned all your life for human love, and you have found it unsatisfying when it has come to you. Seek now the love of Christ, and you will never have to say when you have won it—'what shall I do with it?' Oh, Meta, my sister, this love is yours for the asking, nay, it is yours without the asking, if you will only receive it. Does He not say—'Behold I stand at the door and knock?' Open your bruised and broken heart to Him; admit Him once and for ever, and then you will hear those blessed words—'Your sins which are many are all forgiven you.' 'Enter ye into the joy of your Lord.'"

In the excitement of speaking thus boldly, of delivering—all unworthy as I was myself —this message to a dying and erring sister, I had fallen on my knees by the bed, I had bowed my head over the clasped hands I was holding, and I had not once looked up while my own voice was sounding in the room.

But, with the last words, I felt constrained to turn my face towards Meta's. A hope—I knew not wherefore—had suddenly thrilled through me, and made me expect almost to

see some miraculous evidence of her chains
having fallen off, of her soul having recognized
its acceptance and forgiveness. Those restless
eyes it had so pained me to look into were
closed now ; the whole countenance was
strangely calm and quiet. A second time
I gazed into it fixedly, intently, and then my
heart began to beat violently. I stretched
out my hand for the now flickering candle; I
held it close to the white face upon the pillow. Some strength and courage that were
assuredly not my own, enabled me to do all
this with an outward quietness that was mar-
vellous to me afterwards. I knew that I was
alone with the dead. I remembered, too,
perfectly, that the last corpse I had looked
upon had been the corpse of this woman's
child. In that moment of unnatural excitement I saw the young, fair face of Alan, Earl
of Clinton, quite as vividly and distinctly as
I saw the face of his hapless mother. And
then, by one of those odd freaks that the
mind will sometimes take when it has been

strained to the utmost, the whole of Meta's past life, as I had known it, floated in a clear vision before me. The wasted youth, the degraded womanhood, the sad and bitter ending ere time had planted one furrow in the cheek, or robbed of its gloss a single braid of the shining hair.

She, too, this fair, and beloved, and fascinating woman, had sown to the wind and reaped the whirlwind. According to her own sad confession the human she had chosen instead of the divine had failed to satisfy even the human thirst she acknowledged. Their "wild berry wine" had been dry and bitter to her taste; she had turned from it with a sick loathing; and what remained for her weary heart and soul beyond?

Ah! I dared not follow, even in the most reverent speculation, whither that freed spirit of an erring mortal had gone. Charity itself could only fold its hands in meek silence, waiting, with the patience which God should give, the revelations of that great day when the quick and the dead shall stand before the opened book, and shall be judged " every man according to their works, whether they have done good, or whether they have done evil."

CHAPTER XVII.

ALL'S WELL THAT ENDS WELL.

It was not till many weeks after his wife's death that our poor Guy was in a condition to listen to the united entreaties of his mother, my husband, and myself, that he would come and take up his residence amongst us. Finally he did so, and between us all, by slow degrees, we nursed him into comparative health and strength again. The Guy of former years had of course no longer an existence. Few men could go through what he had done,—no man of Guy's nature, I should think,—and come out of it with very much of his identity remaining. But this was of little consequence except in the estimation of the doting mother, who, fondly as she loved and honoured the grave, joyless, self-sacrificing man she was proud to call her son, could still never quite leave off mourning the loss of the eager, hopeful, enthusiastic boy, she had wept over one summer's morning as he parted from her to begin his career (that should have been so brilliant and successful) at Cambridge.

True, he was even yet little more than a boy in years, and he might, had he chosen, have redeemed the past in every sense that the world could have taken note of. My husband urged him again and again to resume his studies, to be ordained, to adopt the vocation he had originally made choice of. But Guy, grown so yielding on almost every point, was firm as a rock on this. And I think, his arguments were sound.

"I have forfeited my right," he said, "to enrol my name amongst those who publicly serve their divine Master. I turned from His service once, choosing a God that my own hands had made, and I do not feel as if in that way he would accept or bless me now."

But in an humble, unostentatious, and utterly self-forgetting way, Guy did most devotedly and untiringly serve the God he had formerly neglected. In visiting and praying with the sick ; in teaching and ministering to the poor; in all works of charity and labours of love which as a private individual he might undertake, my brother was an example to every one around him. To my dear Harold he became an invaluable assistant; to me and my children he has ever been the kindest and most generous of friends ; to his mother he was and is the support and blessing of her declining years, making the sun as it nears its setting seem brighter and warmer than it ever did in its meridian splendour.

And this is doubly well, since some of us, who pretend to be prophets, anticipate that ere long Mrs. Beamish's eldest daughter may

be asked to leave her quiet duties at Lindenhurst, and assume others which will perchance
interest her more. My husband has at length
succeeded in prevailing on Walter Kenyon to
come and pay us a visit. I should not think
much of this did it stand alone, but when I
add that every six months, during the last
three years, a picture has come from Rome,
addressed to Miss Gertrude Beamish, and
that Miss Gertrude Beamish has not only
accepted these graceful and gracious offerings
but thanked the generous donor of them in
letters for which she has paid double postage,
I do not think I shall be deemed very fanciful
or romantic in the expectation I have expressed. And I sincerely wish I may be
right, for not only do I see that my dear
Gertie requires more than she has hitherto
found to satisfy her heart and render her life
complete, not only this, but my own experience as a married woman makes it
impossible for me to do otherwise than pray

that blessings such as mine have been may descend on all those whom I love.

It is quite true that Walter Kenyon, even did the page of his past life read as fairly and clearly as his present, could never be compared with Harold Wyke; but Gertie would scarcely relish a husband who left her nothing in his character to watch over and help to mend. Her own nature is less fitted to lean upon others than to be leant upon. I believe that she and Walter will do excellently together, and Harold (who triumphs greatly in the growth of that good seed which he ever professed to discover in Walter's heart) believes it and rejoices in it too.

Mrs. Arnott, who came to call upon us a few days ago, having heard of our invitation and its acceptance, said she meant to try her luck again in capturing the charming young man she had formerly so much admired.

" And as widowers, you know," she added, with a nod at me, " are more easily caught than bachelors, I have every hope of succeeding this time."

"And Mr. Leslie?" I laughingly enquired, giving her, as I generally did, measure for measure—"what has he done that he is to be turned over for a younger man, who is far less likely to make a darling of his wife?"

"Oh! Mr. Leslie is a recreant," she replied, with a little frown, and a little tapping of her foot upon the carpet, " and I have changed my mind again about the advantages of being petted by elderly men with grey and scanty hair. You know, Mrs. Wyke, you and I never could agree on some subjects."

My husband had entered the room unperceived as the lively widow was speaking.

"What do you say, Ethel," he asked, drawing me to him in the old, lover-like fashion, when we were left alone. " Have you too changed your mind about the pleasure of being an old man's darling, or are you content with the hard destiny that has been awarded to you, still?"

"You are not an old man, Harold," I replied running my hand lightly through the dark locks in which I saw no more threads of silver than I knew to be in my own, "but old or young I think you do not require me to tell you that to be *your* darling is to me the sweetest, the happiest, and the brightest destiny in the whole wide world."

THE END.

T. C. Newby, 30, Welbeck Street, Cavendish Square, London.